"What do you need?"

The question was quick and impulsive. Her response was even quicker. And bold. Yes, Kris thought as he sucked in a quick breath when she'd taken that step closing the distance between them, it was bold.

"Why?" she asked. "What do you need, Prince Kristian?"

He stared at her for much longer than he figured a smooth and charismatic man should. Then again, those had never been traits Kris possessed. He was the mature prince, the serious one who was all business, all the time. But he'd never done business with a woman who looked and smiled like Landry Norris. None of his dealings were filled with the scent she wore, or the sound of Landry Norris's voice. And nobody, not even the women he'd dated over the years, whether for convenience or for political reasons, had ever made him lose track of what he should be doing.

Yet his response to her was simple and came as naturally as his next breath. Kris touched a finger to her chin, tilting her head up farther. Her lips parted slightly as her hazel eyes stared back at him. He leaned in closer, wanting desperately to see those eyes filled with lust. Wanting, even more hungrily, to touch his lips to hers, to taste the sweetness of her.

Dear Reader,

I am so excited to introduce the glamorous life of the royal DeSaunters family! One of my favorite moments while writing this series was actually cruising to the Caribbean islands and receiving so much inspiration for scenes in this trilogy.

I hope you have as much fun reading about this fabulous family as I did writing about them.

Happy reading,

ac

to Marry a Prince

A.C. ARTHUR

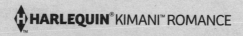

HARLEQUIN® KIMANI™ ROMANCE

Recycling programs for this product may not exist in your area.

ISBN-13: 978-0-373-86497-3

To Marry a Prince

Copyright © 2017 by Artist Arthur

Printed in U.S.A.

A.C. Arthur is an award-winning author who lives in Baltimore, Maryland, with her husband and three children. An active imagination and a love for reading encouraged her to begin writing in high school and she hasn't stopped since.

Books by A.C. Arthur

Harlequin Kimani Romance

A Cinderella Affair
Guarding His Body
Second Chance, Baby
Defying Desire
Full House Seduction
Summer Heat
Sing Your Pleasure
Touch of Fate
Winter Kisses
Desire a Donovan
Surrender to a Donovan
Decadent Dreams
Eve of Passion
One Mistletoe Wish
To Marry a Prince

Visit the Author Profile page
at Harlequin.com for more titles.

To everyone who found their Prince Charming and to those who may still be looking. Dreams do come true!

Chapter 1

He took her breath away, and for Landry Norris, stylist to Hollywood's most glamorous women and debonair men, that was no small feat.

That thought caused the very smooth and elegant curtsy that she'd practiced just before boarding the plane to come off with a bit of hesitation. Still, she smiled brightly as she lifted her head and came to a standing position. He—the Crown Prince Kristian Rafferty DeSaunters—stood before her in all his regal and hot-as-hell glory.

There had been a flurry of activity in the last couple of days, all of which had culminated in this moment. Landry clasped her hands in front of her cream-colored peplum top and gray pencil skirt, hoping she had made the correct outfit selection. That was her thing, after all—finding the right outfit for the right occasion and pairing it perfectly with the person who would wear it. Very rarely was she that person. But Malayka Sampson, one of Landry's newer clients, had changed that.

In her briefcase, which she had left downstairs in the massive marble-and-gold-decorated foyer, was a signed contract between Landry Norris LLC and Malayka Sampson, the woman soon to be princess of Grand Serenity Island. That title and all that went with it had both surprised and impressed Landry when Malayka breezed into her Los Angeles office to share the news. On Malayka's finger was a huge emerald, while the woman's face sported a triumphant smile. Landry figured she'd be smiling too if she were wearing that rock.

Before that, Landry had only dressed Malayka for three functions—the Oscars, which Malayka attended with renowned producer Siegmond Elrey, the Met Gala and New York Fashion Week. Malayka was a cold call client, something Landry rarely accepted. One—she wanted to keep her personal stylist company small and intimate so that she could specially cater to her clients. And two—because most of the cold calls meant she had no idea who the potential client was or what type of funds they were working with.

She'd taken a gamble on Malayka Sampson and it seemed to have paid off, in spades.

"Have a seat, Ms. Norris," the prince said in a low, deep voice that made Landry think of hot baths and back rubs.

She moved carefully to one of the cherrywood upholstered armchairs and gingerly took a seat. Considering Landry was used to being around wealthy people, handling gowns worth more than her childhood home, visiting mansions and attending movie premiers, being a guest in the royal palace on a Caribbean island felt unfamiliar to her. It was new and exciting and just a little bit nerve-racking.

From what she'd seen so far of the palace—it was lavishly decorated and spoke of the wealth and prestige of the people who lived there. Take this office for example, she thought with a quick glance at the floor-to-ceiling windows and grand stately furniture, it was one hell of a space. Roughly the size of the top level of her condo back in LA, the room was meticulously decorated with gold-leaf-framed portraits, Aubusson rugs and a large glossed wood desk where the gorgeous crown prince sat.

"It is Miss? You're not married, are you?"

She could see his lips moving but had been too wrapped in the wonder of her surroundings to pay attention to what was being said.

"Excuse me?" she replied with a shake of her head, a silent admonishment to herself in hopes she would get it together.

He sat back in that dark leather chair, his honey-brown complexion combined with the pale gray color of his Italian-cut suit jacket providing a stark contrast. Behind him the white plantation shutters that covered each window were opened so that slices of sunlight slipped into the room.

"I asked if you were married."

He sounded annoyed but his facial expression remained the same.

Dark eyebrows draped dramatically over velvet brown eyes. His jaw, not exactly strong but precise, just like his nose and ears. It was almost as if he'd had his pick of physical attributes and he'd done an excellent job putting them together.

"No. I'm not married," she managed to finally reply.

A curt nod was the only telling sign that he'd even heard her answer as he immediately reached for a folder on his desk and opened it. He stared down at the papers that she presumed had something to do with her. The amount of paperwork she'd completed before coming there reminded her of when she'd purchased her condo. Grand Serenity Island had a tough security system. She presumed it was that way only for persons who would be staying in the palace, and not for every tourist who wanted to visit this Caribbean haven.

"You've been in business for two years. Landry Norris LLC is the name of your company. You're a personal stylist. So you select clothes for adults to wear?"

He was speaking as if he were reading from cue cards and didn't quite understand what the words meant. It irritated her. She'd grabbed the arms of the chair and squeezed as she restrained the urgency to speak her mind.

When he looked up, his thick, perfect brows raised in question.

Landry cleared her throat, realizing he was expecting an answer.

"I assist my clients with choices that will enhance the way they look and feel. I help them select clothing that will suit their natural features and lifestyle. When a person is looking their best it can be a confidence booster. My job is to not only dress clients, but to assist them in their personal growth."

She spoke succinctly and from the heart. Her job was her passion and while she knew others might not see it as an "important" career, it was hers and she was proud of it. By the time she'd finished speaking her hands were calmly in her lap, her head tilted just slightly as she waited for the prince's next comment.

"Malayka Sampson," he continued, as if her statement had been as interesting as reciting the alphabet. "How long have you known her?"

"Our first contact was via email in late November. She

needed a dress for the Oscars—that's an American award show," she informed him.

"I know what the Oscars are," he countered quickly.

He *would* know, she thought. The royal family of Grand Serenity had been the guests of the president of the United States on numerous occasions in the last eight years. When Landry was inclined to pay attention to the political arena, for reasons other than keeping up with the fashions worn by the First Family and the many dignitaries they entertained, she'd seen Prince Rafferty DeSaunters, the widower who ruled this island, and Princess Samantha DeSaunters a few times. She also remembered another royal sibling, a brother, one who was pictured in magazines and newspapers more often than she'd seen any of the others. But as for this one, the crown prince, the one who would rule the island following Prince Rafferty, she had not seen as much.

The prince continued, "How did she learn about you and what did she ask of you?"

"Another one of my clients had a party and Malayka was there. As I've heard from both of them, my name was brought up in their discussion, and Malayka sent me an email a few days later."

"Why didn't she call you? Did your other client not give her your number?"

"At that time of year I am extremely busy going over resketched gown proposals and backup wardrobe pieces. There are fittings and accessory meetings, as well as lunches with reps of designers I may consider for next year's awards season. My cell phone is always on and always with me, but there are times when I may not be able to answer. My clients know this and have been known to send a text or an email. Sometimes it's easier to give a quick response that way, when I'm unable to speak to them personally at the time."

If this were an interview, Landry might be failing. She was very aware of that fact.

Smile more. Be friendlier. Stop being so defensive.

Those were her mother's words as she warned Landry for the millionth time about finding the right guy.

First impressions are everything.

"How many clients do you have?" was his next question.

Landry resisted the urge to sigh. "Ten."

"So few. Do you plan on expanding?"

"I plan to run a small and personal business, one where I can really get to know my clients and thus provide them with the best service possible."

He looked somber. The expression had not changed since the moment she'd sat down. "And you like catering to people?" He paused. "Why?"

"There are only some people I like catering to, Your Highness. Malayka Sampson is my client and she's hired me to dress her for the events leading up to the wedding. That's the only reason I'm here on your island. And if we're finished, I really must meet with Malayka—we have a great deal to get done before the engagement party."

She'd stood then because sitting was no longer an option. Her hands were now shaking, her heart beating a tense rhythm as she fought to remain calm. When in actuality, she was extremely annoyed. She did not like being questioned as if she were considered disingenuous, or that her business was not up to his standards. Yes, he was the prince of a gorgeous island, but he was still a man and Landry wasn't used to cowtailing to any men, or women for that matter.

He'd surprised her by standing as well. It was a quick motion, one he either hadn't expected to make, or didn't appreciate having to make. As he came around that large desk, Landry remembered the book she'd read on the plane about royal protocol. Most men in America did not stand when a woman did. An attestation to the whole chivalry is dead mantra. Here, the men—correction, the royal men— were different. At least that's what the book said.

"Welcome to Grand Serenity Island," he stated and extended his hand to her.

Landry hesitated momentarily, but then accepted his hand and looked him in the eye.

Did the earth shake? Was that thunder she heard? Who turned up the heat in here?

A wave of heat flowed steadily from her fingers to her wrist, up her arm and rested embarrassingly in her cheeks. He looked down at their hands about a second or so before she did. He was a few shades lighter than her mocha hue.

When she looked back, it was to see him staring at her. She could swear her thoughts were mirrored in his expression. Prince Kristian DeSaunters was not blushing as she feared she probably was, but he did appear shaken. It was a faint change from the stern and serious look that had been in his eyes just moments before. His lips pressed together tightly until he almost seemed to grimace.

"Thank you," Landry replied but made no attempt to remove her hand from his grasp.

His fingers moved over hers as their gazes held.

"No rings," he spoke quietly.

"I'm not married," she answered. "I thought we already established that fact."

Neither was he, Landry thought. He was single and dashing and still holding her hand. It felt natural and odd at the same time. Welcome, yet a bit too familiar for their first meeting. And still, she did not pull away.

"I look forward to seeing more of you," the prince continued. "More of your work, that is."

Right, she reminded herself. She was here to work, not to ogle this man.

"Thank you, Your Highness. I plan to do my very best," she said in her most professional tone, just as there was a knock at the door.

He was still holding her hand when someone entered, already speaking.

"Hey Kris, we need to talk about tomorrow's meeting with the board of directors and then—" her voice trailed off as the stunningly beautiful Princess Samantha Raine DeSaunters came to a stop right beside them.

The prince dropped Landry's hand as if she'd had a palm full of hot coals.

Landry then finished with the roller coaster of emotions brought on by the introduction to Grand Serenity's royalty, bid a quick farewell before making a hasty retreat.

"Who was that and what did you do to run her away like that?"

Kristian stared at the door Landry had just passed through. He was asking himself an array of questions at the moment, none of which he wanted to share with his younger sister.

"That was Landry Norris. She's Malayka's stylist," he replied then moved to stand behind his desk once again.

He closed the file his assistant had compiled on Ms. Norris and her business venture. The picture that was included—the one that had captured him the moment he'd first seen it earlier this week—was tucked securely in the back. That's where he'd finally put it yesterday, when he couldn't rationalize why he kept staring at it.

"You're kidding, right?" Sam shook her head as she

continued to walk into the office, taking a seat in the chair that Landry had vacated. "Why does she need a personal stylist? She already has her hairdresser and makeup artist here."

Kris took his seat. "I was going to ask you that same question… Do you have someone who selects your clothes for you?"

It seemed like a silly question to ask, especially when posed to his sister, who lived in the same house with him. In his defense their *house* was unlike usual homes. It was a palace, after all. Wonderland, that's what Vivienne DeSaunters, their mother, used to call the family home. Located high on the cliffs of Grand Serenity, a Caribbean island just north of Colombia and Venezuela, the royal palace was a sprawling white structure with jutting towers capped in gold domes. It was roughly the size of twenty-five of the homes in the town below, and housed the rulers who had governed the island for the last sixty-five years.

His family resided in a large wing toward the center of the house with the majority of the rooms overlooking the cliffs that fell off into the glorious turquoise sea. Before Vivienne had come to live in the palace windows had been barred and locked, as one of the former rulers, Marco Vansig, had not been a particularly kind man, thus soliciting more enemies than he could eventually ward off. Under Vivienne's progressive and feminine hand the barred windows were removed and replaced with practical weather-resistant glass ones that sparkled and brought in every ounce of sunlight and the island's magnificent view.

Kris's father, Rafe, had the largest group of rooms in that wing of the house as the reigning prince of the island. Kris and each of his younger siblings, Sam and Roland, had their own rooms situated among the areas of the massive dwelling in a way that provided them all with the privacy they seemed to desire. It wasn't easy living under the titles they held, finding solace within the walls of their private rooms was sometimes all they could manage. At least it was that way for Kris.

As the crown prince, the one who would ultimately succeed his father in ruling their country, Kris carried a tremendous weight on his shoulders. One which was now causing a great deal of stress for him.

"I am not your average woman, I suspect," Sam replied to his question with a quirk of her lips. "I love beautiful clothes and accessories, but I like to have the final say in what I wear or purchase for that matter."

She always looked good, Kris thought, as he stared across his desk at his sister—younger than him by six years—looking vaguely amused by their conversation. Samantha Raine DeSaunters was a beautiful woman with her smooth milk-chocolate complexion, and thick coal-black hair. Her skin tone and assessing eyes came from their father, while her outgoing personality and the innate need to take care of everyone around her were undoubtedly traits obtained from their mother.

"I think it's safe to say that you are nothing like Malayka Sampson," was Kris's dry response.

Sam agreed with the nod of her head. "I don't know that there is anyone like her. Did you know that she has already begun planning the wedding?"

Kris sat back in his chair, folding his hands in his lap, a position in which he could easily be mistaken for his father. "The date is set for December first. The date has significance to her and she wants a grand celebration. Those were Dad's exact words."

"And he plans to give it to her?" Sam asked.

"He does."

She cursed.

It was soft and way too dainty to carry much weight, still Kris realized the severity of the situation at hand especially because it made his normally pleasant sister vent in such a way.

Malayka Sampson was engaged to their father. She was a thirty-seven-year-old American who would, in just seven months, become the princess of Grand Serenity Island. As such she would manage Wonderland…no, that was his mother's. It belonged only to her. It always would. Malayka would manage *the palace* and she would take over much of the community and public relations duties that Sam now held. She would become the new face and voice of the island, while his father continued to rule via business and policy the way his father had before him.

"I don't like her and neither does Roland," Sam told him.

Her words came as no surprise to Kris. Sam and Roland tended to agree on a number of things. Kris was the one who was usually treading on the outside of the sibling bond. That was part of his birthright as his father had taught him from the time he'd been old enough to speak. He was the future ruler, thus he had to lead, always.

"She makes Dad happy," Kris replied. "That is all that matters." For now, he thought, wisely keeping that last part to himself.

"She makes me want to do bodily harm and you know that is not my character," Sam added with a slight chuckle.

"I know. But there are more pressing matters at hand. The Children's Hospital brunch is coming up later this week and the Ambassador's Ball is later this month. Is everything in order?"

Sam nodded, looking down at the notepad she'd brought with her into his office. "Just a few final details for each event and they're all set. As I mentioned when I came in,

I have meetings with the board of directors at the hospital tomorrow and after that, I'll be spending the rest of the afternoon at the Bella Club."

Kris nodded as he reached for a pen to make note of his sister's whereabouts the following day. He also had access to her business calendar on the private network the monarch shared. Roland's and Rafe's business calendars were also available to him. However, Sam had a number of personal ventures that meant a lot to her. Kris respected that and envied his sister's passion in helping wherever she could. The Bella Club was an organization Sam had started to offer refuge, counseling and rehabilitation to troubled young adults between the ages of thirteen and eighteen.

"That sounds good," he said as a thought entered his mind. "Would you mind taking Landry Norris with you tomorrow?"

"Who? Oh, the personal stylist?" she asked with a lift of her precisely arched brows. "Why would I do that? She's Malayka's employee, not mine."

"She is a guest in the palace and a tourist. You are on the board of tourism."

"So are you," she countered.

Kris didn't bother to frown, even though he completely recognized the never-ending sibling game that often had each of the royal children pointing out the other's duties to see who had the most on their plate. Kris always won, hands down. Which was why, this time, he was delegating the responsibility.

"I'm meeting with the finance board at nine. That will take up at least three hours of my day. Dad and I then have a late lunch scheduled with Quirio Denton, the real estate mogul who wants to build his next resort here on the island. I won't be available again until dinner," he stated matter-of-factly. "And as you know, because you've been doing this since you were sixteen, it is our practice to provide a detailed tour of the island to visitors of the palace within twenty-four hours of their arrival."

She gave a slight nod. "That's when we know they are arriving and when we've invited them. Malayka hired this woman without consulting any of us. I say let her conduct the tour," Sam rebutted. "It would give her practice since it will soon be one of her duties as *princess*."

That title, above Sam's other words, echoed throughout the room.

"She's not the princess yet," Kris remarked, in a tone that was much stronger than he'd anticipated.

Sam tapped her fingers on her notepad. "Fine. I will take the stylist with me. It'll give me the chance to find out more about Malayka and why she really wants to marry our father."

"I don't know if you'll get much by way of gossip from this Landry Norris. She strikes me as a professional."

"Oh really?" Sam asked, this time leaning forward tossing him a knowing grin. "What else about her strikes you, big brother?"

Kris looked away. He concentrated on the notes he was jotting down, instead of his sister's question, which made him uncomfortable.

"I performed a cursory interview of her. I have a copy of her contract with Malayka and I checked the references she provided. This is how I came to the conclusion that she is a professional."

"Right, because you're very thorough when it comes to investigating who enters these walls. I get that. But what I'm really asking is, what was going on between you and the stylist when I came in? You know, when you two were standing close enough to have kissed."

Kris looked up quickly then, staring at his sister in

shock. Composure came immediately afterward because even with his siblings, Kris had to remain in control. A leader always set an example.

"As Malayka's stylist she's now palace staff. Personal dalliances with the staff are inappropriate."

"Hmm." Sam made a sound and stood with her notepad tucked under one arm. "Tell that to your brother. He's had more dalliances with staff, visitors and whoever else he could find, than the both of us."

Kris made a similar sound as he stood, undoubtedly agreeing with his sister. Roland was another matter entirely.

Sam was almost out the door when she looked back at him and said, "Still, I have to admit the two of you looked awfully cozy and mighty cute together."

She was gone before he could think of another statement of denial where he and Landry Norris were concerned. When he sat back in his chair, he struggled to dismiss any thoughts he'd had when Landry had stood so close to him. When he'd definitely wanted to—against all his training and upbringing—kiss her.

Chapter 2

Classy and elegant, that's the look Landry was going for tonight. After all, it would be the first time Malayka was presented to the entire royal family. Butterflies danced in Landry's stomach as she pushed wayward strands of hair from her face and zipped the back of Malayka's dress.

"There," Landry said, looking over Malayka's shoulder into the floor-length mirror.

It was one of four mirrors which had been sealed together in an arch shape situated at the back of the walk-in closet. Who was she kidding? This was not a closet. The room was at least the size of two bedrooms outfitted with racks for hanging clothes, shelves for shoes, medium-sized drawers for purses and smaller ones for scarves and jewelry. Even with all the items that Landry had brought with her and the ones she'd shipped a week before, there was still a good deal of space before Malayka would come close to filling this room. The dresses tried on tonight were specially ordered designs, four of which Landry would have to ship back to the designers first thing tomorrow morning.

"You look stunning," Landry continued.

Malayka turned to the side. She looked at her plump bottom and rubbed a hand over her flat stomach. Turning again so that she could see herself from another angle, Malayka smoothed her hands over the bodice of the dress. The neckline was cut higher than Malayka was used to but she still seemed pleased. The woman loved to display the cleavage from her size D breasts, something Landry figured Prince Rafferty also appreciated.

"This will be the first time since we've announced our engagement that I've been in a room with all of Rafe's children," Malayka said in that smoky voice that reminded Landry of the time she'd met Grace Jones.

"They'll certainly have to agree that you are more than ready to dress the part of being princess of this beautiful island," Landry told her as she moved away from the mirror and began packing up the other gowns that Malayka had tried on.

She'd been in there for the last two hours trying to figure out which dress Malayka would wear. Luckily, the hair stylist and makeup artist had already been there by the time Landry arrived, so that part of getting ready for tonight's dinner was complete.

From behind her she could hear Malayka making a sound and mumbling something. Landry kept moving. Whatever Malayka had said was apparently not meant for her to hear.

One of the first things Landry learned about working in an industry with wealthy and famous people was to mind her own business. This lesson had come just months after she'd graduated with honors, receiving a bachelor's degree in Apparel Merchandising and Management from

California State Polytechnic University in Ponoma. She'd been ecstatic the day she found out she'd landed one of the coveted internships with *Harper's Bazaar* in New York. There, she had assisted with sample trafficking, creating shoot boards and supporting market editors with office duties. It was just a few weeks after she'd been in New York that Landry met Peta Romanti, the A-list actress who was, at that time, launching her own fashion line. *Bazaar* was doing a full spread and in-depth interview with Peta in the weeks leading up to her launch.

Landry had recognized the woman immediately and used every method of control she could think of to resist acting like a complete groupie. Throughout the day Peta barked orders, sending interns and even editors scrambling to do her bidding. Landry had been busy with other assignments all that morning, but in the afternoon she'd offered to help out during a photo shoot. Happy to have someone else go into the lion's den, Landry's supervisor had given her an armful of dresses and instructions to take into the dressing room and see which one Peta wanted to wear. The actress-turned-designer had decided to capitalize on this interview by modeling clothes from her own line for the spread in the magazine. As she'd walked up to the dressing room door Landry could hear the argument. Something about Peta's boyfriend being arrested for public nudity as he'd stood on a sidewalk arguing with the hooker he'd hired, who he was then accusing of stealing his wallet. Landry stood at the door, not sure whether she should knock and go in, or come back later—even though there wasn't really a "later" since they had already been behind with the shoot.

The decision was made for her as the door abruptly swung open and Peta yelled in her face, "What are you doing there? Are you listening to my conversation? You'd better not speak one word of it!"

All Landry could manage to say was, "I have your dresses if you're ready to try them on."

The afternoon had proceeded with Peta—once she'd asked Landry her name—calling her every five seconds to do any- and everything for her. That day led to Landry being invited to Peta's Paris fashion show three weeks after that and later to receiving personal invitations and previewings to Peta's collection from the moment Landry opened her doors for business. Keeping her mouth shut had been an invaluable lesson and Landry reminded herself of that constantly.

Now well versed in the ins and outs of the personal stylist business, Landry admitted, there wasn't much to be said about Malayka Sampson. She'd been in LA for just about a year when Landry had first met her. When she'd queried her services, Landry had discreetly asked around about the woman, who was neither an actor nor singer, or notable figure. All that could be said was that Malayka had been at all the right parties and premiers. She had dinner with the governor and lunch with a senator. There were pictures of her with record producers and none other than Peta Romanti, which had been the deciding factor in Landry choosing to work with her.

Landry figured that was enough of a platform to style Malayka for the months leading up to her wedding. Add that to the gorgeous scenery that Landry was already aching to see more of, and this was a good opportunity for her career. Her family, however, would say otherwise.

"The men are never a problem," Malayka was saying, loudly this time. "It's the females who are always jealous."

Landry had been closing the box filled with jewelry

she'd brought into the room with her. The sound echoed throughout the high-ceilinged room. She cleared her throat.

"I'll see you in the dining room in a bit," she said as she quickly clasped the lock on the box and picked it up.

The dresses to be returned were all bagged and hung on a rolling rack she'd pushed down the long marble-floored hallway to get to Malayka's private rooms. In her estimate, the palace was roughly the size of at least two Beverly Hills hotels, and that was only a hunch. Earlier that day Landry had been met outside of Prince Kristian's door by a pinch-faced older woman with a heavy accent who escorted her to a room that seemed a couple city blocks away. She figured her approximation was almost accurate.

"You're going to dinner?"

Apparently that surprised Malayka, whose dramatically arched brows were raised as she touched the diamonds glittering at her neck. The woman was just a shade or so lighter in complexion than Landry. They probably maxed out at the same height when neither were wearing heels—five feet six inches tall. She was older than Landry who had just turned twenty-six last week. A marvelous plastic surgeon and a good regimen of weight loss supplements were most likely responsible for Malayka's slim, but stacked, size six frame. Her hair, or rather the expensive wigs she wore, were of the highest quality and were always on point. As was her makeup, courtesy of the other two stylists she'd brought to the island with her. She was perfect to look at, but not the friendliest person in the world.

"Yes. I was told to be ready at six," Landry said as she lifted her arm and looked down to her watch. "I've got twenty minutes to make it or the stern warden lady that gave me the directive might pop a button in that crisp uniform she wears." Landry made sure to chuckle after her words. She wouldn't have the future princess thinking she had no respect for the staff.

Malayka only blinked, the long fake eyelashes fanning dramatically over her smooth skin. "I thought it would be a private dinner tonight. Family only."

Landry nodded and headed out of the closet. "See you in a little bit," she yelled over her shoulder without turning back.

She moved through the sitting area of Malayka's room. It was the size of the entire front end of Landry's studio in LA, plush cream-colored carpet and gorgeous antique furnishings, complete with stunning oil paintings of what she suspected might be the landscape of the island draping the walls. The knobs on the double doors were crystal and reminded Landry of the old doorknobs in her grandparents' house. She was certain these were real, as opposed to the ones Nana used to joke about selling and becoming rich.

When the rack and the other two bags she'd left on the couch in the sitting room were through the doors, Landry turned back and closed them with a quiet click. Then she sighed. The last couple of hours had been taxing but worth it, she supposed. Malayka did look good and that was her sole purpose for being there, so she whispered a *job well done* to herself and headed back in the direction she'd remembered traveling to get there.

These were the glossiest and prettiest floors she'd ever seen and Landry had been to a lot of sophisticated venues. Nothing compared to this palace. The word *palace* alone meant this place was classier than anything she could ever imagine. It was certainly living up to its hype, and she was only in the hallway.

Columns jutted from the floor to the ceiling, some wide, some slim, all giving an air of royalty as she moved through. What seemed like secret alcoves encased sculptures of pirates and ships. Closer to her rooms there were busts of people she was sure she had never heard of, but who nevertheless looked extremely important. The color scheme here was the barest hint of peach flanked in beige-and-gold textured wallpaper, highlighted again by the swirling marble floors. There were large floral arrangements on small round tables; the tropical plants added bursts of colors and scents as she moved through the area. Every few feet or so, the walls would break to an opening that displayed a gorgeous mermaid sculpture and fountain in its center. This one showcased a courtyard that had access to the outside so sun and sea-salted air filled the atmosphere.

It was just around the corner from that courtyard that Landry's rooms were located. Yes, she had a sitting room, also a private bathroom, bedroom and balcony. The space was elegantly decorated. She probably could have comfortably stayed here during the times she was not taking care of Malayka. The stern-faced lady had told her that she could simply pick up the phone on her nightstand and dial zero for assistance, which included having meals brought to her room. Free room service in a royal palace; for a second, Landry thought she could get used to living like royalty.

That thought had her chuckling as she entered her suite, pushing the clothes rack to the much smaller walk-in closet she was using for some of the items she'd preselected for Malayka. There was a coat closet and another enclosure, which she figured was supposed to be a linen closet. But Landry had decided to store her own clothes here.

She rushed into the bathroom to shower and slip into the dress she'd already chosen for herself. Being a college student and working two jobs, added to the two years she'd spent in New York when her internship had been extended, had taught Landry how to dress in a hurry. She lined her eyes, stroked on mascara and added a bit of color on her eyelids. The quick makeup routine stalled momentarily when she discovered she was getting low on her favorite lip gloss. It only took another second or so for her to browse through her makeup case and settle on a nude gloss instead. Swiping that on quickly, she found her earrings—silver buttons that matched the bangle she pulled onto her arm. Slipping into five-inch-heel sandals was next before standing again and grabbing a random bottle of perfume and spritzing herself generously. Her hair was already up in a messy bun and once she looked into the mirror, Landry decided it was the perfect accent to the otherwise neat and almost demure dress she wore.

It was navy blue, with a layer of lace over the tight bodice and full asymmetrical skirt. There was also a slip to the dress, crinoline, the most despised fabric in Landry's opinion. Still this dress needed that extra poof to the skirt. As she stood looking in the mirror, moving from side to side the way she'd seen Malayka doing, Landry thought she looked like the twenty-first-century Audrey Hepburn. She smiled because she liked it.

Moments later she was leaving her room, only to come face-to-face with a man who looked nothing like the dour staff worker who had promised to escort her to the dining room. No, this was no older person. He was young and built and wore the white dinner jacket and black pants like a seasoned model. His face was breathtakingly handsome and when he smiled, Landry almost swooned.

"Ms. Norris. I would be honored to escort you down to dinner," he said with an extravagant bow.

When he was once again upright, Landry touched the sides of her dress and curtsied—because something told her this guy was royal. He had to be. He was too beautiful to be just a mere human.

He was reaching for her hand when she straightened.

"I am Prince Roland DeSaunters, and it is my immense pleasure to meet you."

No, Landry thought as she let him take her hand in his and they began to walk down the hallway, the pleasure was definitely hers.

The table could easily seat somewhere around fifty or so people. It was huge and a glossed cherrywood. A pristine white runner stretched its entire length; gold candelabras held tall white candles with golden flames at their tips. Ornate brass chandeliers hung from the high ceilings while several matching sideboards filled the great space. Beneath the table was a plush rug decorated in deep reds, greens and of course gold. But the definite eye-catcher to this room was the enormous arched window situated perfectly behind the head seat of the table. The window had automatic shades that Landry suspected were room darkening as well as provided privacy when needed. The shades were raised tonight so that the last intense colors of sunset over the glistening water were visible.

As if this room and its awe-inspiring view weren't enough, the rest of the royal family was seated at the table and now staring expectantly at her.

Landry already felt a bit lightheaded by the gorgeous man walking beside her and the scent of his intoxicating cologne. Prince Roland had talked the entire time they walked, commenting on the very statues she'd perused not long before. He laughed a lot which made her smile. He walked with a seasoned swagger that said he knew he was not only good-looking, but rich and powerful and none of that meant a thing. She liked him instantly.

As for how she felt about the rest of the family, well, nervous or not, she was about to find out.

"Heads up," Roland said as he continued to guide her down the length of that table to where the others were seated. "Gang's all here!"

As they approached, Prince Kristian stood and so did his father. Seated next to Kristian was Malayka who looked at Landry with her brow raised in question once more. She was most likely wondering why Landry was arriving with Prince Roland. Landry was wondering that herself. The princess sat opposite of Malayka, her expression more amused than questioning.

"Ms. Norris," Prince Rafferty said as he stepped away from the table to stand in front of her as she approached. "It is a pleasure to meet you. Kristian has told me all about you."

Landry did another curtsy—she was getting really good at them now. The prince took her hand, kissing the back of it in a gallant and romantic gesture that stole her breath and made her smile.

"The pleasure is all mine, Your Highness. Thank you for having me in your home. It is a beautiful palace," she said then snapped her lips shut for fear of babbling.

"You are welcome here for as long as Malayka requires your assistance."

His response was more formal than the slight lifting of his mouth as if he were contemplating a smile.

"And this is my sister, the Princess Samantha DeSaunters," Roland announced after turning her once again toward the table.

His hand was lightly touching her shoulder. Landry looked at the princess. In Landry's line of work, she was used to seeing beautiful people—whether it be natural or assisted via surgery, hair extensions, makeup, designer clothes, whatever it took. This woman was actually very pretty, the light makeup and lovely ivory-colored gown she wore only adding to her allure.

Her complexion was a little lighter than her father's, her dark hair curling to her shoulders. Her eyes were intelligent and assessing and the smile she gave Landry was, thankfully, genuine. So Landry mirrored it.

"It's a pleasure to meet you, Your Highness."

"Very nice to meet you, Landry. Kris also told me a lot about you."

Well, Landry thought with a tight smile as she gazed across the table to "Kris." He had been talking about her a lot, hadn't he.

"And you've already met my older brother, Kris, next in line to rule this magnificent island," Roland said as he began guiding Landry to the seat between the princess and another empty chair.

Prince Rafferty had already taken his seat and Kristian was now watching her with an obvious frown as she sat in the high-backed cushioned chair Roland had offered.

"There will be a bridal party meeting on Friday. Everyone that I've selected will be flying in on Thursday. I'm thinking that a lovely breakfast on the north terrace would be nice because there's not much sun on that side of the palace that early in the day," Malayka began speaking, once everyone was seated and servers had arrived with plates of a colorful salad.

"The Children's Hospital brunch is Friday at eleven," Samantha announced, her tone just shy of being frosty.

"Oh," Malayka said, her fork poised over the salad she was just about to dig into. "Well, the palace is enormous, I'm sure we can entertain two groups at the same time. Isn't that right, Rafe?"

"The royal family is expected to attend the brunch.

The Children's Hospital performs in a professional manner throughout the year and is the top medical facility for children in the Caribbean. This is our way of thanking them for a job well done."

Kristian spoke with an air of finality. There was no mistaking his authority, not in his tone, nor in the way his shoulders squared. He wore black. His suit jacket had satin lapels, and his shirt had a white silk tie at the neck. It was a decidedly Mafia look to Landry's eye, but it worked exceptionally well with his buttery complexion. His hair was jet-black, just like the rest of the royal family, but cropped closer than Prince Rafferty's and Roland's. Where Roland's low-cut beard gave him a rugged, handsome quality, Kristian's clean-shaven face suited his dour expressions perfectly.

"Well, I've already made the plans. Everyone is preparing to travel. It's not possible to cancel at this late date," Malayka implored.

The look she was giving Prince Rafferty was almost comical, but Landry knew not to laugh. This was, after all, serious business for the soon-to-be princess. Malayka undoubtedly expected her husband-to-be to stand up to his children in front of her, to let them know that she was getting ready to be the one wielding all the control. Landry should have felt uncomfortable being privy to this private duel of sorts, especially considering she was only the staff. Malayka's makeup lady and hair stylist weren't at this dinner, which would explain why Malayka had been surprised that Landry had been invited. Landry wondered about that too, but the salad was delicious, so she really didn't want to wonder too much.

"We will work something out," Prince Rafferty stated in his deep, booming tone. He also gave Kristian a look that said they would definitely *work it out*, later.

Kristian showed no emotion at all. He proceeded to cut through his salad, lifting measured forkfuls to his mouth to be chewed.

Roland picked that moment to chuckle. "Just let me know which event I'm required to attend. I'll be flying out Friday evening."

"Really? I did not see that on the calendar," Prince Rafferty said to his younger son. "When will you return?"

Roland shrugged and forked a bright red tomato into his mouth. "Don't know."

Prince Rafferty wiped his fingers on a napkin then placed the white cotton square down on the table slowly. "The engagement will be officially announced tomorrow. There will no doubt be press arriving on the island within hours of the news circulating around the world. We all need to be on hand for official photos and interviews."

Landry thought about that statement as she chewed the last bite of her salad. She did not recall seeing any interviews of Prince Rafferty in any of the American papers. Of course she hadn't actually searched for any either.

"You're giving interviews?" Samantha asked. "You never give interviews."

Malayka reached a hand out to rub along Prince Rafferty's arm. "This is the age of social media. We—the royal family—should be as transparent as possible at all times," she told them.

Kristian set his fork down slowly and looked directly at his father.

"The exposure the wedding will elicit for the upcoming months will no doubt improve tourism on Grand Serenity. The more tourists that visit the island, the more money the shop owners in the village will earn. The more money they earn, the more jobs they can provide. It is a win-win situation for all of us," Prince Rafferty stated.

He'd looked around to each of his children, an effort to gain their support, Landry supposed. However, she wasn't certain it was going to work. None of them seemed thrilled about this idea.

"Sounds like you two have this all planned out," Samantha replied.

"Not all," Prince Rafferty continued. "The press conference needs to be arranged for tomorrow morning at ten."

"We have a meeting at the bank tomorrow," Kristian interjected. "It's on the calendar."

Rafe nodded as the next course of their meal arrived. It looked like chicken and vegetables in a dark sauce and it smelled fabulous. Landry immediately picked up her knife and fork and began to cut into the boneless breast.

"You handle the bank meeting and I will stand by my bride-to-be at the press conference. Roland, I want you there, dressed in full regalia and a smile on your face. Put that on your calendar and do not be late," Rafferty said sternly.

"Yes, sir," Roland replied with a salute to his father and a nod to Malayka.

"And you, my Sammy," their father continued giving a much softer look and tone to his only daughter. "I don't want you to feel as though you were left out of the loop on this. Malayka and I just talked about this last night. Furthermore, I would think that you, above everyone else, would be happy to see that Malayka is perfectly able to plan with our island's best interests in mind. She's going to make an excellent princess and I have no doubt she will continue to have this palace running like a well-oiled machine, just as you have."

Samantha did not look impressed. However, she did smile and nod to her father and then, to Landry's surprise, to Malayka as well.

"I look forward to the day when I can hand off a good portion of my duties to you, Malayka. I just hope you know what you're getting into," Samantha said as she lifted her glass of wine and did a solo toast toward the couple.

Landry couldn't help herself, she grinned at the sarcasm in that moment. Sure, it was cleverly masked, but there was no doubt in her mind that the princess was anything but happy about having soon-to-be Princess Malayka taking over anything in the palace.

"We are amusing our guest," Prince Rafferty said.

Landry coughed immediately, embarrassment almost choking her.

"Well, we aim to please here at Grand Serenity Island," Roland added and lifted his glass, mirroring what Samantha had just done to Malayka.

As for Kristian, the scowl that had graced his face from the moment Landry had walked into this room was still perfectly in place as his gaze settled on her.

"I apologize," she said when she was certain her words wouldn't come out in a jumble. "I meant no disrespect. It's just that this scene reminds me of my family. I thought I was going to miss them terribly but it was nice to have this little reminder."

It wasn't a total lie, Landry told herself. She did come from a large family. Her parents had lived in the same house for the entire thirty years they'd been together. And as of ten years ago, her paternal grandparents had also lived in that house, along with Landry's four brothers, sister and her two kids. So yes, she was used to hostile family dinners, just not on a royal scale.

"Well, glad we can entertain you. But I suspect your stay here will also be educational as you watch a new leadership take the reins."

The prince was talking about Malayka, which, for

reasons Landry could not actually put her finger on, she thought was hilarious. Malayka Sampson was going to be a princess. Just five short months ago when Landry had first met her, she was introduced simply as an entrepreneur. Seems like Malayka had found her next business venture. Or perhaps she'd actually fallen in love with a real-life prince. How coincidentally wonderful for her.

"Yes, sir. I believe my time here will be interesting," Landry found herself saying instead of what she was really thinking.

"Interesting indeed. I mean, wouldn't you be anxious to get the ball rolling if you were going to run a Caribbean island?" he asked her.

Landry shook her head. "I'm not sure that would be something I'd be interested in doing, Your Highness."

"Really?" he asked as he sat back in his chair, wineglass in hand. "Are you saying you would turn down an invitation to become princess of this island?"

In a heartbeat, Landry thought.

"Yes, sir, I would. I'm not princess material."

Chapter 3

What is she doing here?

Kris asked himself this several times throughout the dinner. She'd walked in with Roland, arm-in-arm, both of them smiling, looking picture-perfect. He'd frowned.

He had felt his forehead wrinkling, his teeth clenching. Beneath the table where his hands had been resting calmly on his thighs, his fingers had slowly curled into fists. Why did they look like they belonged together when they'd only just met? Or had they?

Roland was his younger brother. He wasn't the immediate heir and so he did not have the duties and responsibilities that Kris had, nor did he express any interest in them. Instead, Roland's goal in life was to see just how much fun he could have before he dropped dead—at least that's what he'd always told Kris. Lately, with all the traveling Roland had been doing, combined with all the gambling and sleeping around with the woman of the month, Kris had begun to believe his brother was more than serious about achieving his life's goal.

That only made seeing him with Landry more annoying.

But it shouldn't have. He didn't know this woman, not well enough. Everything he'd read on paper about her schooling, where she lived in America, what she did for a living, had all been superficial. Kris had no idea who she really was on the inside and thus could not accurately pinpoint her motives in coming here. But there was a motive, he was sure. Everyone had a motive or a master plan.

Especially Malayka Sampson.

When the meal was thankfully over and second rounds of Chef Murray's crêpes Suzette had been devoured, Kris stood, eager to excuse himself. His plan was to retreat to his rooms, to the solitary space he craved so much after a long day of doing his job.

The job that hung around his neck like a heavy chain.

"Well, I'm off for the night," Roland announced as he, too, stood after dropping his napkin to the table. "It has, as always, been a pleasure. But duty calls."

Kris didn't bother to hide his displeasure. "Duty?" he asked and looked down at his watch. "It's almost seven thirty. What business do you have at this hour?"

"Don't you mean what date does he have at this hour?" Sam asked with a smirk.

Roland had already moved from his spot and was now leaning over to kiss his sister's offered cheek.

"Ha ha. And they say I'm the funny one," Roland joked.

Sam took the hand that Roland had rested on her shoulder, squeezing it gently before saying, "Be careful."

"Yes," Rafe began after loudly clearing his throat. "As I mentioned there will be members of the press lingering about once our engagement is announced."

Roland and Kris shared a look. Kris stood slowly and Roland gave a stiff bow to his father, his smile still in place.

"I hear you loud and clear, Dad. But the announcement isn't until tomorrow. That gives me plenty of time to get into as much trouble as I possibly can before then." Roland wiggled his brows as he finished and Kris felt compelled to step in before his father lost his patience.

"I'll walk out with you," Kris announced and then looked to Rafe. "You and I can figure out a time to meet tomorrow after your press conference and my meeting at the bank, but before the meeting with Denton. Good night, everyone."

It was easier to be formal, Kris thought to himself as he recalled Roland and Sam's warm exchange. This relieved the tension of knowing that he would never kiss Malayka's cheek or smile warmly at her. Roland didn't care about how that could be construed to the one person at the table who was an outsider. His brother simply acted, consequences would come later, those that Roland would likely ignore. Kris, on the other hand, did not ignore consequences or repercussions. He was duty bound to consider them with everything he did, from the clothes he wore to the way he pronounced a person's name. He was always under the microscope. Always expected to do and say the right thing.

"Let's go," Roland said after smiling and giving another bow to Landry.

Kris nodded curtly in her direction and found her staring at him after she smiled up at Roland. He chose to walk away then because he did not like how looking at her made him feel.

"She's a looker, I know," Roland said the moment they were out of the dining room.

Their dress shoes clicked somberly on the floors as

they walked toward the foyer. Roland was already unfastening the top button of his shirt. It was as close to being dressed for dinner as his brother had ever deigned to become. While Kris and their father wore a suit and tie, as was most usually their attire, and Sam dressed elegantly as always, getting Roland in slacks, a dress shirt and jacket was as good as they could manage.

"She's working for Malayka," Kris reminded his brother. He did not want to think of how she looked.

"Yeah, that's kind of strange, but then I guess not. That woman acts like an American superstar. She's had an entourage with her since the first time she set foot on this island. And Dad lets her have whatever she wants," Roland stated. "What do you think about that?"

Kris shook his head. "I'm trying not to think about it," he lied. "We're about to conduct the yearly audit on the banks. A few of the board members are nervous about one of the accounts. I've been looking into it, but I want to play it close."

Roland chuckled. "Don't want to step on any toes, huh, big brother? You'll tread lightly with the bankers, just like you will proceed with extreme caution where this royal wedding is concerned." He clapped Kris on the back. "I'm so glad you were born first."

Kris stopped walking just as they approached the double staircase in the family wing of the palace.

"You're still a member of this family, Roland. You still have duties and responsibilities to the monarch. The people of our country still depend on you," Kris told him in a serious tone.

"They depend on me to entertain them," Roland said. "I give them relief from our stuffy family filled with traditions and pomp and circumstance. I breathe a breath of fresh air into this stately fortress and stern but compassionate rule of the DeSaunters family. Don't be dismayed, Kris—I know my role in this family and I play it very well."

He did, Kris thought. Roland played his part perfectly and sometimes, for just a few hours out of a month or possibly year, Kris wished he could be as laid-back and carefree as his brother.

"We do not need any bad press right now," Kris said, shifting gears slightly. "Whatever you're up to tonight, keep it discreet."

Roland pulled off his jacket, holding it by a finger as he tossed it over his shoulder. "Don't I always?"

They both shared a knowing look then, before Roland laughed and Kris reluctantly cracked a smile. He loved his brother and his family, he truly did. That's why his job was so important. Everything he did was for them, for their country.

Once Roland was gone, Kris stood looking around at all the gray-streaked white marble, the shining columns and sprawling staircase. He looked up to the domed top of the room that was painted with puffy white clouds and a soft blue background. He had no idea whose concept that was but suspected it was meant to make a person standing there feel better. Though, for him, it didn't. Every day couldn't be a beautiful and picture-perfect day.

"It's beautiful," he heard her say and slowly tore his gaze away from the ceiling.

"The murals and sculptures I've seen in the palace so far are simply stunning. I'm not usually an art buff, but I know what looks good."

She continued to talk as she walked, her high-heeled shoes clicking over the gleaming floors. Her dress was drastically different from the formfitting outfit Malayka wore and was certainly more intriguing. Kris found himself staring at—of all things—her shoulders. They were pretty, her skin tone the perfect shade of brown, and appeared smooth to the touch. To the taste, he thought as he wondered about kissing her there. He would drag his tongue slowly from one shoulder to the next. Would she tremble beneath him? Would his mouth water? It already was.

"I've never seen a place like this before," she said, reaching her arms behind her back and clasping her fingers together.

Her hair was dark and pulled up so that her slender neck was visible. She walked slowly from one part of the room to the other, looking at things that Kris had seen so many times he could describe them each while blindfolded.

"I should probably head back to my rooms, but every time I come out I see something different. Something more beautiful," she said.

"There is nothing…" Kris said impulsively. Nothing more beautiful than her, he thought, but wisely, did not finish his comment.

She turned then, facing him with her head tilted slightly. "Excuse me?"

No, Kris's mind screamed. No, he would not excuse her and as he was already walking toward her, he apparently would not stay away from her either.

"There is nothing here that you cannot look at as long as you like," he told her. "As a matter of fact, I've asked my sister to give you a full tour of the island tomorrow."

"Oh," she said, seemingly surprised. "I'm only here to work. I don't mean to take up any of the royal family's official time. Besides, I'll be with Malayka early tomorrow morning until after the press conference."

He stopped only a few feet away from her. He was so close he could smell the soft scent of whatever fragrance she wore. It wasn't the powerful come-get-me scent that he'd smelled on so many women he'd met. No, this was lighter, with a sweet, musky aroma instead of a heavy floral one. He liked it. A lot. He also liked how she was looking up at his six-foot-two-inch frame now.

"Sam will be attending the press conference as well. The two of you can leave afterward," he stated.

Then Kris did something he rarely ever did while in someone's company. He slipped both hands into his front pant pockets. It was a casual stance, one that did not equate to the role of a leader.

"I wouldn't want to impose," she said.

Her voice had changed. It was subtle and he doubted even she realized it, but Kris did. There was a smoky tinge to her words and just as he made that realization, she licked her lips. His body tensed.

"She's the president of the tourism board—it's her duty to welcome all tourists to the island," Kris told her and instinctively took another step closer.

"Why?" she asked and he paused. "Why did you ask her to show me around? You know I'm not technically a tourist. I'm here to work for Malayka."

"I know why you're here."

"Then why did you insist I come to dinner? You did that, didn't you? The housekeeper—"

"Ingrid," he interrupted.

She nodded. "Ingrid said I was supposed to be ready at six, that I was expected at dinner. She was in the hall waiting when I left your office earlier today, as if she knew I would be coming out. Why didn't you invite Malayka's hair stylist and makeup artist? Why only me?"

Kris did not have the answers to any of her questions. Another first for him. He had instructed Ingrid to tell her about dinner. All he'd known at that time was that he'd wanted to see her again. Just as he hadn't been able to stop looking at her pictures all week, Kris now couldn't keep his eyes off her. While his more official thought had been that he wanted to know everything there was to know about Malayka's staff, it was Landry, in particular, who had awakened something in him.

"You don't care for dinner? Is that why you're questioning me?" he asked.

She smiled then, a slow and deliberate action.

"You don't want to answer my question," she said. "That's fine. Still, I don't want to impose on anyone. I'll do some sightseeing whenever I'm not working, but I don't think I need a guide."

"What do you need?"

The question was quick and impulsive. Her response was even quicker and bold. *Yes*, Kris thought as he sucked in a quick breath when she'd taken that step closing the distance between them, *it was damn bold.*

"Why?" she asked. "What do you need, Prince Kristian?"

He stared at her for much longer than he figured a smooth and charismatic man should. Then again, those had never been traits Kris possessed. He was the mature prince, the serious one who was all business, all the time. But he'd never done business with a woman who looked and smiled like Landry Norris. None of his dealings were filled with the scent she wore, or the sound of Landry Norris's voice. And nobody, not even the women he'd dated over the years, whether for convenience or for political reasons, had ever made him lose track of what he should be doing.

Yet, his response to her was simple and came as naturally as his next breath. Kris touched a finger to her chin, tilting her head up farther. Her lips parted slightly as her hazel eyes stared back at him. He leaned in closer, wanting desperately to see those eyes filled with lust. Wanting, even more hungrily, to touch his lips to hers, to taste the sweetness of her.

He shouldn't.

He couldn't.

He was a breath away. She leaned into him, her arms remaining straight by her side. Her lips were still parted, her tongue beyond them, teasing and tempting him.

He was the crown prince. She worked for the woman who planned to marry his father.

He couldn't.

Kris closed his eyes and leaned in just another inch or so, until her warm breath smelling of the sweet crêpes they'd just had for dessert fanned over his face. He inhaled the aroma, feeling the heat of desire swelling in the pit of his stomach.

What was she doing? Was she completely out of her mind?

Why on earth had she thought the crown prince of this beautiful island would want to kiss *her*? They'd only met hours earlier. It was ridiculous. Presumptuous and possibly career ending if she were to be kicked off the island. Malayka was exactly the type to spread vicious rumors. And since this one would have a great amount of truth to it, Malayka would happily report back to everyone she knew in the United States.

Landry sighed, letting her head lull back against the door to her room, which she'd slammed closed and locked a few minutes after she'd left Prince Kristian and run all the way to her temporary sanctuary.

She was such a screwup.

Impulsive. Headstrong. Opinionated. Mouthy.

All words Landry had heard before in reference to her personality.

"Men don't want women who push too hard, Landry. They want someone agreeable and calm spirited."

Those were Astelle Norris's famous words to her daughter. They were famous because she'd spoken them more times than Landry could count.

"Wives are submissive to their husbands," Astelle would continue as she sat at the kitchen table doing some chore she thought wifely. Like snapping green beans for dinner or sewing socks so that her husband Heinz Norris's toes wouldn't poke through as he stood in the pulpit of the Baptist church where he pastored.

Landry could feel her eyes rolling back in her head as she recalled one of the more popular disagreements she'd had over the years with her mother.

"I'm not doing any man's bidding. He can cook just like I can and he can go out and buy himself a new pair of socks if his have holes in them. I don't have to be subservient to get and keep a man," was Landry's typical response.

Astelle, with her thinning, but still long silver-gray hair, only shook her head. *"It doesn't make you less of a woman, Landry. It makes you a* good *woman."*

"To who?" Landry had asked. *"If I give a man that much control over me, who am I any good to? My future daughters will only see that their mother is so fragile and clueless that she can't do anything without permission from a man? My future sons will grow up believing they rule the world, not for their brains or intuition, but because they have a penis so it should be so?"*

In a rare display of anger, Astelle had stood quickly, dropping the beans she'd held into a large yellow bowl as she glared at her daughter through tired gray eyes. *"I've never been clueless, Landry Diane Norris. I graduated at the top of my class at Brighton Business School and I worked in a law office for the first five years of my marriage until my husband finished school and received his PhD. I came home and started a family where I took care of my children and the head of my household. Six productive and intelligent people were brought into this world because of me and all the lessons I've taught them. My husband is a pillar of this community. He's a teacher and a confidant and a good provider. I'm just as proud of him as I am of our children. So don't you stand there after another failed relationship and pretend to know what my life has been like or what may have been better for me. I won't stand for your disrespect."*

By the time her mother had finished speaking her hands were shaking with rage and Landry felt like crap. Astelle had left her in that kitchen alone, where Landry spent a few more moments wallowing in guilt and wondering how long she should wait before apologizing to her mother. Her father had come in during that time, rubbing his hand over Landry's head as he used to do when she was a child.

"Put your foot in your mouth again, huh, pumpkin?" Heinz had asked with the booming melodic voice of a southern-born minister.

"Yes, sir," had been her quiet response.

"She's only telling you what she's learned. That's a mother's job," he said as he went into the refrigerator and grabbed a bottled water.

Landry watched her father's strong hands—the same ones that, when she was ten years old, had fixed the chain on her bike—twist the cap off the water before lifting the bottle to his lips and taking a gulp. She saw the man who had carried her mother to the car the night she'd awakened in pain and stayed at the hospital every second Astelle was there having her emergency hysterectomy. Landry had only been sixteen then. He was the same man who had placed money in Landry's hand and told her to go to the grocery store and get some things to have cooked before Astelle came home. The man who had written check after check for Landry to attend college when the scholarships she'd received had run out.

"I'm not the type of woman she is," Landry had admitted. *"I could never be like her."*

Heinz shook his head, his short-cropped black hair having long ago made the transition to snowy white. *"She doesn't want you to be like her. She just wants you to be good and true."*

"To bow to some man and say what he wants to make him happy. Kevin Blake cheated on me with a freshman that had big boobs and a fake butt. What could I have done to make him happy if that's the kind of trash he wanted to chase in the first place?"

"Nothing. Because he was a jerk. But not all men are and your mother is simply trying to prepare you for a mature and fulfilling relationship."

"She's trying to make me a Leave It to Beaver *wife in the age of* The Real Housewives.*"*

Heinz chuckled then. *"Now, those women, you should definitely take note of."*

Landry had been surprised by what her father had said in reference to the reality TV series. But more so because as she'd been talking to him, she'd moved to the seat that her mother had vacated and started snapping the green beans and dropping them in that same yellow bowl.

"You're saying I should take advice from the housewives?" she asked because that made more sense than trying to figure out what she was doing with the beans.

"No," Heinz replied with a hearty chuckle. *"Not at all. What your mother and I have built over the course of our*

marriage is something special and sacred. It's also been very rewarding for us. Of course your mother would want you to find the same type of commitment for your life. The thing is, what I think you're missing about the type of marriage that your mother and I have, is that it's rooted in love. Your mother could not do and say the things she did with regard to our marriage if she didn't love me with every fiber of her being. For that I am forever grateful as there is no greater love on this earth. As for me, I can only thank the Lord daily for the blessing of my wife. I love her phenomenally and I cherish her. That's what she wants for you, Landry. That's what we both want for you."

Well, that was never going to happen, Landry thought as she pushed away from the door and stepped out of her heels, kicking them across the Aubusson rug.

She reached behind and unzipped her dress as she walked toward the rack where she'd left the hanger. Landry stood in the middle of the fanciest room she'd ever had the pleasure of staying in and stripped the expensive dress off her body. She hung it on the rack once more, traipsed over to the bed and plopped down onto the shiny cream-colored comforter.

She'd thought for sure Kristian wanted to kiss her. Everything about him said so. The way he'd stepped to her and touched her chin. His eyes had grown darker, his lips parted. Well, hers parted first because not only had she assumed he wanted the kiss, she'd been anxious for it as well.

With a heavy sigh she fell back on the bed, one arm going over her eyes, her hand to her stomach as if she could possibly calm the butterflies that still danced happily there. She wanted to kiss the prince. Not the sexy flirtatious one that probably would have easily taken her into his arms and kissed her senseless. No, she had to want the other one. The one who looked at her like she was no better than the rug he stepped on. She hadn't been here a full twenty-four hours and already she was messing up.

But tomorrow was another day and she needed to get an early start. Malayka was going to be anxious and irritable. Everything would need to be perfect for her first official appearance as Prince Rafferty's fiancée. So with a resignation to keep her mind on things that it should be on, Landry moved over the bed until she could push down the comforter and slip beneath it and the sheets. Lying on a soft pillow she stared up at the ceiling and attempted to think of the dresses she would pull for Malayka tomorrow. The shoes, earrings, necklace, rings. How her hair would be styled. Makeup soft, or bold?

Those thoughts were quickly replaced by the sights of the windows across the room. Large windows, no curtains, giving a clear view out to the night sky. Dark, but with tiny pricks of light. Stars, Landry thought. There were stars out tonight. What would happen if she wished upon a star?

Not a damn thing, she thought with a chuckle. This wasn't a storybook and wishes did not come true. Sure, she was lying in a king-size bed, in a room in a palace. Tomorrow morning she would watch a prince announce that he was about to make a woman a princess. A woman, who for all intents and purposes, came from the same place that Landry had. And yes, tonight she'd dined with said prince, plus two more and a princess who smiled easily but managed to run their household and island in grand style.

There was still reality. The one where Landry was a business owner and Malayka was a client. She would do this job and then she would return to LA, to her family and her condo. To her world. The princes and princesses would all remain here in the land that looked to be fresh out of a childhood storybook, but had no place in Landry's dreams.

Now that was a buzzkill if ever she'd experienced one.

Landry turned on her side, closed her eyes and forced them to remain that way. She thought of dresses again, of colors and materials. She did not think about Kristian, or his lips, or how a kiss from him would have tasted. She refused, and that took way more energy than planning a wardrobe for any client ever had.

Chapter 4

Kris watched the taped version of the press conference for the third time. There was a throbbing between his eyes as he hit the stop button on the remote, ending the recording seconds before turning the television off.

He was in his rooms now, two hours after his meeting at the bank had ended. His second meeting of the day had been cancelled and his father had never contacted him about when they would meet today. Kris sat back in the leather chair in the sitting area that he'd turned into an additional office and stared down at his desk. He did not have time for this.

Press conferences about wedding plans, announcements about parties, and yes, the blatant disrespect Malayka had just shown to the local dressmakers, were all among the things Kris did not want to deal with. There were too many more important things for him to occupy his thoughts with.

The meeting at the bank and the concern that had been gnawing at him for weeks, for instance.

Grand Serenity Island was an independent territory that had been acquired by the Netherlands in the 1600s. The island did not flourish as the early settlers would have liked because of its dry climate and thus the lack of agricultural prospects. That began to change in the late 1800s when the son of a British sailor named Montgomery Chapman decided there had to be more to this place than gorgeous waters and warm air. Montgomery and his group of slaves discovered the Rustatian Gold Mill, which eventually went on to produce three million pounds of gold. In the immediate years following, the island saw more growth in the building of its first oil refinery, which was also owned by the Chapman family.

By the time Kris's grandfather, Josef Marquise DeSaunters, gained control of the island via his leadership role in the rebellion against the then ruling tyrant, Governor Marco Vansig, the gold mills and oil refineries were the island's main sources of income. However, Vansig's greed and vicious rule had burned many bridges in the trade industry, leaving Josef with no other option than to look for additional opportunities for the citizens of the island to continue to thrive. On the advice of his wife, Josef formed the island's first tourism board and by the early 1980s, when the oil industry began to wane, tourism became Grand Serenity's financial savior.

It was Kris's father, Rafe, who came into rule after Josef's death from throat cancer. Rafe vowed to continue his father's vision for the island. Rafe knew the value of forging strong partnerships on and off the island. This led him to venture to the United States where he met with potential developers and owners of the burgeoning cruise lines. This was also where Rafe met his wife, Kris's mother, Vivienne Patterson, whose father was a Texas oilman.

Kris dragged a hand down his face at the thought. His chest clenched and he spent the next few seconds tamping down the well of emotion that always swelled when he thought of his mother, who had died when Kris was ten years old. When Kris was certain he could concentrate on the pressing matter at hand once more, he opened a large file filled with papers he'd brought back with him from the bank and began sorting them into three piles.

As a young man during his father's rule, Rafe had begun to amass more fortune for the DeSaunters family by constructing financial institutions. He'd been successful with soliciting wealthy international clients, as well as celebrities, to invest and bank with Grand Serenity as a way of remaining ungoverned by their country's financial restrictions. This had been the first aspect of governing the island that Rafe had taught Kris. From the time Kris was a young boy, his father had talked of the banks and how they, along with the tourism, would sustain the island's growth, even as the natural resources continued to dwindle.

Thus came his degree in international finance. Kris spent numerous hours a day poring over financial reports and statements from each of the three banks on the island.

Three months ago, Kris had received reports of two new accounts that had been opened with multimillion-dollar deposits. The accounts had continued to see hefty deposits in the following weeks. This alone did not raise any red flags, however it was the signature cards on the account that did.

A. M. Belle Vansig.

The name had immediately struck a chord in Kris's mind, yet when he'd searched deeper into the account, he hadn't found any further identifying information for this person.

"You're not concerned?" he'd asked his father during one of their morning meetings.

"It's just a name, Kris," Rafe had responded as he'd scooped spoonful after spoonful of sugar into his coffee.

The strong and stern ruler of the great Grand Serenity Island had a vicious sweet tooth.

"A name that has meaning in our family's past and the history of this island," was Kris's counter.

Rafe shook his head. "Marco Vansig and his army were conquered by my father and his soldiers. Their bodies were burned at sea. Vansig had no wife, no children, nothing but his precious gold, which was turned over to the island treasury department upon his death. He was a dark spot in this island's history and then he was gone. Now, decades later, you see the name and what? You think Vansig is reaching up from the grave to cause more mayhem?"

Kris had to admit that the idea seemed far-fetched. There were numerous people throughout the world with the same name that had no connection to each other whatsoever. Still, he'd decided to keep an eye on the accounts anyway.

"Nonetheless, I've been thinking we should implement a more thorough background check for new account holders. With the rise in criminal activity connecting to offshore accounts, we want to be sure that we're working on a higher level."

"Our institutions are not founded on the rules and regulations of other financial facilities. This is why we are able to hold such lucrative accounts. We do not overly tax our customers with paperwork and supervision of their own funds," Rafe had immediately rebutted.

"I know that we are not regulated by such organizations as the United States Federal Reserve or the European Commission and other such places throughout the world. Our customers run from Russia to South America and we retain their autonomy and confidence by not working in any fashion with these other regulating entities. But that does not mean we do not have our own regulatory process. We should still know who we are doing business with."

"We do," Rafe insisted. "There is no need to change the protocols we have in place. It has been working for years."

"Things change, Dad," Kris told his father. "You know that as well as I do. I'm just trying to look out for our future. It's my job."

Rafe hadn't disputed that fact. His father had been the one constantly drilling into Kris's head the importance of his job and his duty. Kris would rule this island and continue what his grandfather and father had built before him. He would not fail. He could not fail.

Just as he could not bring himself to kiss the sexy American last night.

There had been no other reason but his duty. She was a very attractive woman, with a personality unlike the many women who had crossed his path. With Landry Norris there were no pretenses. She had not come into his office batting her eyes, or crossing her bare legs for his perusal. Her reason for being here had been perfectly explained by all the paperwork she'd completed and the way she'd sat across from him answering his questions, even though she thought they were over-the-top. Of course, she hadn't said that—which showed that no matter how honest she seemed, she did have respect for his position. Kris could tell by the way she'd watched him carefully after providing each answer. She'd wondered if the answer was good enough for him, while inwardly not caring because she told herself she had no intention of answering any other way. Her subtle boldness and their conversation had been intriguing to Kris.

So much so, that at last night's dinner he'd found himself watching her, listening to her talk and laugh, more focused on her than all the business issues that he still had to deal with. Kris had no idea when something else had taken over his mind before business.

Last night, she hadn't shied away from him. He hadn't really expected her to; he was the crown prince, after all. Not that he was conceited in any way. To the contrary, Kris wished on more days than he could count that he were just a regular guy. If he were, then he could have kissed her last night and maybe there could have been more, like a long evening in bed, a slow start to the morning after waking with her in his arms.

He sighed heavily and then shook his head. Thoughts like that were for other people, in other places. Not him and definitely not here.

"Nice to see you made it back from the bank in one piece."

Kris looked up to see Roland walking into his private office. Kris hadn't bothered to lock the doors since he was expecting Roland. Besides, his brother rarely knocked on any doors in the palace. Roland Simon DeSaunters always had to make a grand entrance. Their mother used to always tell the story of the night of the Ambassador's Ball when she was barely seven months pregnant and her water had broken as soon as she and Rafe made their entrance into the ballroom. Roland had been born one hour after that moment, yelling at the top of his lungs, announcing his arrival as if they hadn't already known he was coming. Vivienne had always smiled when she retold that story. Rafe, on the other hand, would frown. Their father had frowned a lot where Roland was concerned.

"Nice to see you made it to the press conference and on time," Kris replied.

He was finished removing the papers from the folder and set it to the side on his desk.

Roland closed the office door before taking a seat across from Kris's desk.

"I said I would be there," he told Kris.

"You did."

"I always keep my word," Roland continued. "You know that."

Kris nodded as he looked over to his brother who was now dressed in khaki pants and a polo shirt. Kris couldn't remember the last time he'd been able to dress so casually.

"You are trustworthy," Kris said. "Even the billionaires you swindle out of their money can attest to that."

Roland shook his head. "You've got it all wrong, big brother. I do not swindle. I play cards and I play them well. Those with huge bank accounts and even larger egos should never underestimate that."

His brother was smiling. Kris was not. As long as Kris was alive and well, he was next in line to rule. Roland was not. As such, he hadn't been trained and groomed the way Kris had. That was not to say that Rafe hadn't raised both his sons with a strong and firm hand, because he had. There were rules and they were all expected to follow them because Rafe's wrath was nothing to be laughed at. Sam had been handled differently, still, unshakable integrity and dedication to their island was a given for each one of them. Roland was the only one who did not agree to those terms.

"So that's where you're off to tonight. I saw on the schedule that you're leaving town today and will return in time for the brunch on Friday, before taking off again Friday night. You're going to join in another one of those poker games aren't you?" Kris couldn't hide the disappointment in his tone.

Roland only shrugged. "You run the banks and stand by Dad looking all dour and debonair. Sam smiles prettily at the tourist board meetings. She is the face of the island, a beautiful Caribbean goddess is what I've heard her called. Me, I'm the recluse. That little bit of danger that intrigues the world and probably draws in quite a bit of tourists as well. Just like the Americans who flock to Hollywood to see the homes of the stars," he said with a chuckle. "It's what I do and, just like you and Sam, I do it well."

"Regardless of the repercussions?"

"I'm an adult, Kris. I went to school and graduated just like Dad had commanded. He said since I did not care to attend college like you did, that I had to enlist in the military. The Royal Seaside Navy was less than happy to put up with me for four years, but they did and I completed my time there. I've done my part."

"Have you, Roland?" Kris asked as he leaned forward on his desk. "You don't help with any of the business of this island. Sam and I both carry more of a load than you. Hell, you barely show up for dinner or other functions. You know you're not doing your part."

"I'm doing the part that fell on my shoulders. If my big brother weren't so perfect and my younger sister so pretty, maybe there would have been something left for me. Alas, I'm not into complaining. I'm making the best of my situation."

"I'd give you any one of my assignments if you acted halfway interested," Kris admitted.

Roland drummed his fingers on the arms of the chair. "Thankfully, I'm not. And this isn't the real reason you called me. So why don't we skip the rest of this conversation because we already know how it's going to end."

Kris frowned. He hated when Roland was right.

"Were you paying attention at the press conference this morning, or did you just show up to be seen?" he asked after taking a slow, steady breath and releasing it.

"I heard every word, just like everyone on this island and probably a good portion of people across the world did."

Roland lounged back in the chair.

Kris rubbed a finger over his chin. "Sam doesn't care for her."

"And now, neither do the dressmakers on this island. She basically told them she'd attend her own wedding naked before employing one of them," Roland stated.

Kris looked at his brother again. Candor was one of Roland's strong points.

"Sam cleaned it up well at the end, but I don't know if that's going to be enough. We should do something more," Kris stated.

"Like what? Buy a dress from all the local dressmakers? Aren't the house staff uniforms already manufactured locally?"

Kris was surprised that Roland even knew about the house staff uniforms at all. "Last night you were talking to Malayka's stylist. The two of you seemed...friendly," Kris stated, ignoring the tinge of irritation he felt at the thought.

"Yeesss," Roland drew the word out like he was more than satisfied with the memory himself. "Landry Norris. She was interesting."

Kris didn't need his brother to tell him that. Landry was so interesting Kris had spent a good portion of last night thinking about her when he should have been preparing for his meeting.

"Her job is to advise Malayka on what to wear. What if she suggests a local dressmaker, maybe not for the wedding gown but for something else? It would go a long way for community relations."

Another shrug from his brother. "I guess."

"I want you to suggest this to her," Kris told him.

"Me?"

"Yes, you."

"Why me?"

"Because you think she's interesting, remember? And judging by the way you were looking at her last night, I don't believe it a hardship to ask you to speak with her once more."

Kris's hands had fallen to the arms of his chair, fingers gripping the edges, without thought. Roland leaned forward, resting his elbows on his knees as he stared long and hard at Kris for endless seconds.

"Sam said you told her to take Landry on a tour of the island," Roland began.

"That's correct. As you stated, Sam is the face of the island. People expect to see her out and about especially when guests are at the palace."

"Then why not have her suggest the dressmakers to the royal guest?"

"She might. I know that Sam uses a couple of the local dressmakers herself. I'm asking you because I want to make sure the stylist takes the suggestion seriously," Kris stated.

"The stylist," Roland repeated with a nod. "Her name is Landry Norris. I know you never forget a name, yet you haven't said hers once."

Kris's teeth clenched. "I have these mountains of paperwork to go through today, Roland. Then I have to meet with Dad to brief him and attend yet another dinner with him and Malayka. I'm asking you to do one thing for me and this island's economy. Can you please just take

a moment out of your busy social schedule to accommodate me?"

Roland chuckled then. He stood, nodded. "Sure thing,
big brother. Who wouldn't do the crown prince's bidding?"

The sarcasm wasn't lost on Kris, but he wasn't in the
mood to address it. He had other work to do.

"Thank you," Kris said, moving in his chair so that
he could turn his attention to the paperwork on his desk.

"No problem. I'll make sure that Landry Norris knows
what the crown prince wants from her…"

Kris's head snapped up at Roland's words but his
brother was already gone, closing the door with a definite click behind him.

Chapter 5

His body reacted first.

A jolt of lust so quick and potent Kris almost had to cough to keep from choking. The strong scent of chlorine burned his nose as the balmy temperature from the inside pool area warmed his cheeks.

This was where his training in control and temperament came into play. When he was young, Kris had taken riding, fencing and piano lessons. The latter was because his mother was determined to teach her children something other than duty.

A sword could cut deep and painfully if Kris wasn't in complete control of his own weapon, if his mind wasn't totally focused on the matter at hand. That was the lesson his father had wanted him to learn from the eight-week-long fencing class. There was never any real threat of Kris having to decide local policy via a sword fight. He would, however, need the control and steely resolve of a good leader to face any potential opponent.

In all probability, this learned control and decisiveness was not intended to spill over into Kris's personal life or feelings, but it had. Hence the reason he was now clenching his fists so tightly, the blunt tips of his nails attempting to bite into his skin.

The glistening pool water cast her body in a dreamy seductive haze as he watched intently. She swam gracefully in long measured strokes from one end of the pool to the other. Her bathing suit was yellow, like the sun. A swatch of material covering her backside and a strap crossing her back that he presumed held her ample bosom in place. That was all he saw, other than skin.

Back and forth, Kris watched as she swam, stopping only a few seconds at each end of the pool to take in air. She was counting, he realized after a few more moments of watching. Each lap she did counted toward her goal. He wondered briefly what that goal was and then silently commended her for striving for it in the first place. He also thanked her immensely for her choice of swimwear as five laps later, she climbed out of the pool, giving him a full, unfettered view of deliciousness.

She was curvier than he'd presumed. Generous breasts, full waist, glorious hips and thick thighs. His mouth went dry, his erection hard and persistent. Water rolled off her gorgeous brown skin in slow drops that made him thirstier than he'd ever been before.

At his sides, Kris's fingers unclenched, his palms tingling with the urge to touch. He could see his hands on her waist, holding her close to him, close enough so that he could rub his erection against her. Kris blinked at the abrupt eroticism of his thoughts. It was unlike him, and yet it felt as natural as breathing.

She was coming closer, as he stood only a few feet away from the row of chaise lounges along the side of the pool room. Her hair was slicked back from her face, dripping more water onto her body. Kris wanted to catch every drop, with his tongue. She leaned down to pick up a towel and then stood straight once more. He moved quickly, ducking behind the column that thankfully hid his Peeping Tom presence.

For a few still moments Kris did not move. She knew someone was there. She just didn't know who. This may have been the only cowardly act of his life, but regardless, Kris walked quickly away.

It wasn't until he was locked in his rooms that he thought no, this wasn't the first cowardly move he'd made, but it would most certainly be the last.

"I apologize," Samantha DeSaunters stated the moment they were closed in the backseat of the car together. "I meant to meet up with you last week but my schedule changed abruptly. When I had to change the time of the Children's Hospital brunch to accommodate Malayka's bridal party meeting things sort of spiraled out of control. I'm just getting back on track."

Landry sat back against the cool leather seat, resisting the urge to sigh. It was barely noon and already it was extremely warm on the island. Her nightly swims had been extended to early mornings as a way to cool down. She'd just returned from meeting with Malayka to go over her schedule for next week when the princess had knocked on her door.

"No apology necessary, Your Highness. I've been doing a little sightseeing on my own when I can," Landry said just as the car began moving.

"That's right, Kris did mention that Jorge had taken you

out a few times. Jorge is used to driving the palace guests, visiting dignitaries and such," Samantha said. "And we're alone now, so please call me Sam."

Landry smiled over to Sam and gave her a cordial nod. "Okay, but really I don't need a personal tour. I know that you're all very busy with your own jobs. During the time that I'm here and not working with Malayka, I can certainly entertain myself."

"Nonsense," Sam told her. "You get the royal treatment just like any other guest of the palace. Now, Phillipe is my driver and while he might look tall and a bit scary at times, he's a big ole teddy bear. He's going to take us into town, where I have a quick appointment, and then we'll walk the streets for a bit before having lunch at my favorite place. Afterward we'll spend the afternoon at the museums and we'll be back at the palace in time for dinner."

It sounded like a full day, which coincidentally happened to work well for Landry since Malayka was leaving that afternoon for a weekend trip with the prince. Landry had spent a good portion of her morning with Malayka selecting outfits for the trip. The prince had instructed Malayka that none of her staff could join them and Landry had mixed feelings about that declaration. On one hand, she could certainly use a few dinners without the tension that drifted like heat waves between her and Kristian. On the other, Landry could also use some time away from Malayka who had changed from the budding socialite Landry first met in LA to full-fledged princess mode, even though the title was still months away from being solidified.

"Each one of you have your own driver?" Landry asked to distract herself from thoughts of both Malayka and Kristian.

"Yes," Sam replied. "Rex is my father's driver. He's the palace transportation supervisor. There are five other full-time drivers on staff. Dante is Rex's right hand, so he's been taking care of Malayka's car service needs. Kris's driver is Tajeo and Phillipe sticks with me."

"What about Roland?"

Sam shook her head. "Everybody asks that question at some time or another. What about Roland? Why isn't he coming to the Ambassador's Ball? Why doesn't he stay in the palace as much as the rest of the family?" Sam chuckled then. "Roland is his own man, as he likes to tell us. He drives himself, except when my father insists he act like a royal prince should."

"And how often is that?" Landry inquired with a hint of humor. She liked Roland and his easy smile even though she hadn't seen much of him in the last week.

"Not often," was Sam's reply in a tone that said she liked her brother a lot.

Landry could tell. There was definitely love in this family, even if it was rather stilted in presentation. Landry came from a tight-hugging, wet-cheek-kissing, boisterous family where nobody ever doubted they belonged; everyone felt loved. At the palace, she thought, Prince Rafferty was a serious and domineering father and leader. His children respected him and stuck together because it was what they were taught to do. Love was there, but on well-laid-out terms and with the restrictions of the royal crown. It was as sad as it was a privilege.

"He reminds me of my brother Dominic. He's the second oldest of my siblings and acts like he could easily be the youngest. I call him courageous and adventurous, but my dad insists the correct description should be childish and irresponsible," Landry spoke comfortably as she looked out the back tinted window.

They were riding in a Mercedes-Benz C450 AMG 4matic. Landry only knew this because Dominic loved cars and since she'd always been madly in love with her older brother, she'd stuck to him like glue when she was a little girl. Thus, her own interest in cars had bloomed. It was white with dark tinted windows. She'd seen another one a couple days ago when Dante had brought her back to the palace, so Landry assumed the palace had a fleet of them. She tried not to be awed by that fact.

"Really? How many brothers and sisters do you have?" Sam asked.

Landry turned to look at her then. She was a lovely woman with her pecan skin tone and curly shoulder-length hair. Landry would have to spend at least an hour with the hot wand if she wanted her hair to have lush curls like that. Sam's were natural, Landry suspected, just like her thick, elegantly arched brows were and the exotic tilt of her eyes.

The princess wore a navy blue silk polka-dot dress with a sweetheart neckline, a bodice with gathers and bows at the shoulders. It was a vintage-style dress, circa 1940s, Landry deduced. There was a layer of tulle on the underside to give the dress a full-skirt appearance and her white platform pumps had navy blue polka-dot bows at the tops. It was both lovely and classic and Sam DeSaunters wore it well.

As for Landry, she also wore a dress. A strapless black-and-white-striped one with a cinched waist and fitted asymmetric skirt. Her sandals had one strap around the ankle, one across her toes and a four-inch heel. Sam had a large-brimmed white hat sitting daintily on the seat between them. Landry hadn't thought that far ahead so she'd probably be scorched by the Caribbean sun today.

"There are six of us, four boys and two girls. I'm next to the youngest," Landry told her. "We grew up in a big house that still seemed too small when we were all at home and getting into each other's way. Makes me wish I'd lived in a palace instead."

Of course she'd been joking. Landry loved the old ranch-style home her parents still owned. Five years ago they'd built an addition so that Landry's maternal grandparents could move in. By that time, Landry had been happy that she'd had a place of her own, but still enjoyed going back frequently to visit.

"Palace life isn't all it seems at first glance," Sam replied.

"Most things aren't," Landry told her.

Sam smiled then and nodded. "I think I'm going to like you, Landry Norris."

"These fabrics are gorgeous," Landry exclaimed as she ran her hands over silks in rich jewel-tone colors and vibrant prints.

"We have it imported here for special orders," the woman who Sam had introduced as Detali told her. "The Ambassador's Ball is soon."

"You're absolutely right, Detali," Sam said as she moved about in the shop that did not look large enough to hold a tea party, let alone produce dresses. "It's in five weeks and I haven't even thought about what I'm going to wear."

Detali, a woman who stood maybe four feet nine inches tall, and had the straightest, blackest hair Landry thought she'd ever seen, nodded at the princess. "It is late for you."

"I know," Sam continued. She picked up a large-brimmed black hat with a huge red bow around the rim. Removing the white one she wore, Sam tried on the black hat and looked as stunningly gorgeous as she did in the first one.

Landry returned her attention to the lovely cream-colored satin with the intricately designed turquoise flowers. "This would look lovely on Malayka. She mentioned the ball and we brought some gowns with us, but yesterday she was talking about something different, bolder."

When she was met with complete silence, Landry looked up to see Detali and Sam exchanging a look. "What? Did I say something wrong?" she asked. "Is there a special dress code for the ball that I'm not aware of?"

Sam had replaced the black hat and was now smoothing down a few of her curls. "No dress code," she said as she crossed the room to stand closer to Landry.

"At the press conference last week, Malayka indicated that she did not believe any of the local dressmakers could master her style," Sam told her in a hushed tone.

Landry knew firsthand how selective Malayka was about designers. Even with Landry lending her expert advice, Malayka often had trivial excuses for not using a particular designer. "She smokes, so I don't want her designing my clothes." "Her nails are too short." "He has a unibrow." On and on until Landry had begun to present the outfits before giving Malayka the name of the designer, in the hopes that she'd like the clothes so much that the other ridiculous reasons or rejecting them would be dismissed. That's why, even though Landry had also been present at the press conference and had heard Malayka's comment, she simply planned to ignore it. "Does that mean I could not commission a dress to be made for her anyway?"

Sam lifted an elegantly arched brow at Landry's question, the corner of her mouth tilting into a smile. "You are her personal stylist."

"I am and I usually know what will look good on a client before a client even decides it's worth trying. These colors will look great with her complexion. If we could get the right design, this gown would be stunning."

Landry had returned her attention to the material, unfolding it and laying it over the table where she'd been standing. She thought about an A-line gown, something simple, yet chic and daring in some way. It would need to be regal as was the mood they'd decided to portray for Malayka. The wedding gown was already being designed by Peta, as a personal favor to Landry, and also as another boost to Peta's already stellar portfolio. But for this event, the one where Malayka would be meeting the ruling parties from other islands and countries, she should be breathtaking as she stands beside her prince.

"If I brought you some sketches do you think you could come up with something in time?" Landry turned to the front desk that looked more like a hunk of a tree trunk with its top smoothed over, dropped down into a corner. Detali had to be sitting on a stool now because she seemed taller as her wide eyes fixed on Landry.

She looked from her to the princess in question, before opening her mouth to respond.

Landry wanted to say that she was the one in charge of Malayka's wardrobe and that if Malayka was too stubborn to wear it, Landry was certain she had another client back in the States that she could pair with the gown. Either way, Detali was sure to receive more exposure if she agreed, and if Landry was successful in not only commissioning the gown, but also having it sold to a celebrity in the States, then it was a win-win for them all.

It took every ounce of control that Landry had to keep her mouth closed and look to the princess for a response.

"I think it would be a fabulous idea for the soon-to-be princess to wear a gown from a local dressmaker to the ball. With your name attached to the press that will undoubtedly spread from the prince of Grand Serenity's first official event with his American fiancée, more Americans may seek one-of-a-kind attire from Grand Serenity. It is good business for the island as well as your client. Don't you agree?"

Landry smiled as she realized Sam had been thinking along the same lines as she had. Part of her wondered if that was the reason for this little trip here today, but Landry was too excited by the prospect to give it too much thought.

He was sick.

What he was doing was ridiculous.

This was his house. His island. He could have any woman he wanted, whenever he wanted her. That was a fact and not just some colossal stroke to his ego. Kris liked to deal with facts and truths; unshakable reality was where he preferred to live and function.

His mother used to tell him stories at night before he fell asleep. Some were fairy tales that always had happy endings. One night, when Kris was five years old, his father had entered his bedroom just as Vivienne was telling Kris the story of the prince who rejoiced after finally finding his perfect princess. Rafe was furious and demanded that Vivienne cease telling "his heir" these types of stories because a head full of fluff was not what was going to lead his island to greatness. The next night when Vivienne came to tuck Kris in—and as he'd waited patiently for her to begin another story about some faraway land where love was able to heal all wounds—he knew immediately that the next story would be different.

The stories Kris received that night and many nights thereafter were ones of wars won by the strongest and the smartest. Sure, there might be a kiss here or there, or even a damsel in distress at some point, but the core of every story had been the same—honor, integrity, loyalty. Until the words were branded in Kris's mind and his soul.

So it was reasonable that he stood there, in the pool

room that was closest to the center courtyard of the palace, watching as he had done in the last five or six nights. It also made sense that he would lose count of how many times he'd stood there or how long he'd spent thinking about seeing her when he was away. It was all totally realistic. Wasn't it?

Kris let the question remain unanswered as he slipped his hands into the front pockets of his tan dress pants. He still wore his suit jacket, but it was pushed back up his arms. The sage-green tie that seemed calming against the bright white of his shirt was hidden from view by the wide column in front of him. There were a dozen columns along the perimeter of the pool room, separating the white-tiled floor leading to the pool and the elevated section covered in a glossy black marble flooring where a row of chaise lounges sat.

He had always stood behind this one because it offered the best view of the entire length of the pool. Her bathing suit tonight was gray with pineapples all over it. That shouldn't have turned him on, but at this moment Kris wanted nothing more than to taste a fresh, sweet pineapple dripping juice on his tongue and slipping softly into his mouth.

"Why don't you come on in and join me this time?"

The sound of her voice halted Kris's salacious thoughts.

When a wet hand touched his, he realized she'd gotten out of that pool and walked right up to him without him even knowing. So much for being an astute leader. If she were an enemy she would have had the knife embedded in his gut by now. His teeth clenched with the displeasing thought.

"Come on. It's late so I'm sure you're finished with work for the day. A swim would be nice and relaxing. That's why I try to squeeze this in at least once a day," she was saying as she'd already started walking.

Kris followed her because he hadn't had a minute to think of what else to do. She was in front of him, seemingly pulling him along. But Kris never followed anyone. He was a leader, had been since birth, that was a fact.

"Since I've been here on the island I've managed two sessions in this fabulous pool per day. And let me tell you it's been heaven. The pool in my building back in LA is nice, but this scenery combined with the lingering scent of the ocean is total bliss," she continued and stepped up to walk them past the chaise lounges.

There were doors along this wall that led to changing rooms and extra swimsuits for guests.

"Now, I haven't had a chance to get down to the beach, but judging by that view from my room, that water is going to be heavenly. Maybe when Malayka goes away this weekend I'll have to trot myself on down there to try it out."

She stopped then, right in front of one of the doors and looked up to him. Her hair was pulled up in a messy, wet bun with straggling pieces dripping down onto her shoulders. Her face, free of all makeup was perfectly round. Long eyelashes and pretty eyes, pert lips, high cheekbones, were like nothing he'd ever imagined. Yet, every night this was the face he saw before he fell asleep and each morning it was the one he wanted to see as soon as he awoke.

His thoughts startled him because up until this point, Kris hadn't dared consider it a fact.

"I'm sure you have swim trunks in your room, but it's closer to just go in there and grab some that'll fit so we can dive in," she said to him. "I'll wait right here."

He continued to stare at her, watching as her lips moved and her eyes smiled back at him. She was genuine; at this very moment she wanted him to take a swim with her, and Kris, well, he wanted something...different.

Reaching around her he opened the door to the room. Then, he wrapped an arm around her waist and began walking forward, forcing her to move backward.

"Wait...what?" she was saying as he maneuvered her into the room and closed the door behind them.

The lock sounded loudly as he clicked it into place and the smile in her eyes disappeared. It was replaced by something that had Kris growing warmer, instantly.

"You wanted me to take off my clothes. Isn't that correct?"

His question was spoken in a deadly serious tone, his heart beating wildly as he moved closer to her. She moved back until she was against the mirrored wall, shaking her head as she continued to stare at him.

"I was only suggesting you get changed into swimming trunks so that you could go for a swim," she told him.

Kris took off his jacket, extending his arm a bit so that when he dropped it, the material landed on one of the two oak benches instead of the floor.

"Right," he told her. "Well, let me just take off my clothes so that I can slip into those swimming trunks."

She swallowed so hard Kris could actually hear the action. He was removing his tie now and her gaze had dropped down to his fingers.

"You're a grown man—you don't need any help changing your clothes," she said before clearing her throat.

After the tie landed on top of his jacket, Kris immediately began unbuttoning his shirt, first at the cuffs and then down the center. She looked up to him then, determined to keep her gaze on his face. That was fine with him. For now.

When he was bare to the waist, Kris stepped closer to her. "I think I have a better idea than the pool."

"The pool was what I offered. Nothing more," she said definitely.

He continued moving until the tips of her breasts covered scarcely by the wet material of her bikini top touched his chest. It was a scorching dollop of pleasure. The thought of her nipples just on the other side of that material, probably hard and aching for his attention, had him aching, as well. Yes, he admitted to himself, he wanted her to want him as ferociously as he needed her right now. It was all that mattered, all that he cared to think about at that second.

Chapter 6

Again, Landry had quite possibly gone a little too far. She'd known Kristian was watching her for the last couple of days. While underwater one evening she'd caught a glimpse of his silhouette, but when she'd surfaced it was gone. Throughout the rest of the swim she'd continued to stare in that same spot, feeling as if he was still there even though she hadn't seen him again. The next night she'd heard him approach and had a giddy kind of pleasure at knowing that he was watching her.

Did he want her?

Could the prince want to get into this pool with her, and maybe, want something more? Like what? She'd thought about that the next night and then the following night. What could Kristian DeSaunters possibly want from her? Okay, well that was a silly question. He was a man and she was a woman. Sex was the common denominator and Landry could accept that. But she wasn't too keen on Kristian's official title and her temporary employment on this island. The two didn't match up as seemingly sensible as the sex part did.

Yet, here she was, in this small room with him so close and his chest so bare. The air seemed thick as she struggled to breathe in and out, slowly, precisely. It was the only way to keep her mind clear, to focus on what she should do… rather than what she so desperately wanted to do.

"Touch me," he said.

No. Landry almost gasped as she realized those words weren't just a statement. They were a command.

Her mouth suddenly went dry as her gaze involuntarily dropped to his bared chest. His very toned and muscled chest. She had to admit, that in his suits, Kristian did not look as buff and chiseled as he apparently was. Her fingers tingled with the urge to do exactly as he'd instructed. Yet, the part of her that she'd been frequently warned about would not go peacefully into bliss.

"How do you know I want to touch you?"

She'd never seen Kristian smile, but the corner of his mouth twitched and she thought she would lose control if his full smile was as potent as the seriously sexy glare he was giving her now.

He lifted a hand to touch a strand of her wet hair. "I know that it is taking every ounce of your restraint to keep from doing so because your fingers are clenching and unclenching. I know that feeling very well. I've felt it each night I stood watching you."

Well, Landry thought, *that clears up the whole spying because he wants me theory.*

"I also know that it makes more sense for us to get this out of the way sooner, rather than later."

While his previous comment had sent pleasure shivers racing down her spine, this later one irritated her.

"Like a task on your agenda?"

"No," he said in a husky whisper as he stepped closer and let the fingers that had been toying with her hair trace a warm path along the line of her neck. "Like a thirst that must be satiated."

Okay, she could relate to that.

Landry swallowed and shook her head slightly.

"I'm not…" She paused and cleared her throat. "We're not in a position to…um, do this. I mean, I don't think it's proper protocol or whatever."

His head had already begun to lower, his lips brushing lightly over her forehead as she spoke, then moved down to touch the tip of her nose.

"I'm the prince. I create the protocol," he whispered softly over her lips.

The kiss was probably meant to be sweet and seductive. Perhaps a prelude to a long, languid evening of lovemaking, if she were so disposed to believe in such things. Instead, it turned into a fiery duel of tongues and tangle of arms as they gripped each other and held tight, as if this were not only a quest to quench a thirst, but an actual fight for survival as well.

His bare chest pressed against her almost naked one and Landry's blunt-tipped nails dug into the skin of Kristian's shoulders. Moments ago she had been cool from stepping out of the water into the air-conditioned room; now her entire body was warm, growing warmer. Kristian was not only a prince, but he was also a master at this kissing thing. His arms had folded around her back, pulling her up so close to him that only her toes remained on the cool tiled floor. Her head had long since tilted as to offer more access for his delicious assault, her breasts rubbing seductively against him.

It was as if he were attempting to devour her and to her own bafflement, she was offering herself up to him like a buffet feast. In fact, when his hand moved down to cup her butt, she took the initiative and lifted her leg until her inner thigh ran slowly over the material of his pants.

He groaned.

Yes, the crown prince of Grand Serenity Island groaned because she'd brought her leg up and was now wrapping it behind his back.

His hands moved quickly. One holding her firmly in his grasp while the other slipped between them as he undid the buckle and zipper of his pants.

This was not happening, she thought, even as she pressed closer to him. Not close enough because the ache that now throbbed between her legs persisted. This could not be happening.

It should not be…

She moaned when her back was flattened against the mirror and he sucked seductively on her tongue. Her arms were wound tightly around his neck, holding him in place because she wanted more. She knew he did too. His hands were finished moving between them; his length was hard as it pressed against the bare skin of her lower abdomen. He pulled slightly away so that they could both catch their breath. It was a momentary separation as the kiss ensued once more. Their wild abandon filling the room with moans and sighs and guttural urgings.

"I want you," he whispered.

"I want you," she echoed him.

Then suddenly, without preamble, they both stopped. She stilled and he did too. There was no more kissing, no more moaning, only breathing and thinking.

Too much thinking.

Kris loosened his hold on her. When her feet were firmly on the floor, he stopped touching her and backed away. All the while avoiding another glimpse of himself in the mirror directly behind her.

It was there that he'd been reminded, once more, of what he could not do.

He turned his back to her and began fixing his clothes. She did not move but Kris would swear he could hear her thinking, wondering, most likely as angry and confused as he was at this moment. He owed her an explanation and an apology. When his pants were once again in right order, Kris reached over to the bench and pulled on his shirt. He buttoned it as rapidly as he could, desire to get this over with as quickly as possible.

Not for his sake. No, he was thoroughly disgusted with himself for what he'd allowed to happen, what he'd instigated. But he was more disappointed with how he'd treated Landry, a guest to the palace and someone who worked for them.

"Why?"

She asked in the middle of Kris's mental recriminations. How did she know? Of all the questions in the world, how could she grab hold of the one he definitely did not want to answer? The answer to his questions did not matter. Kris knew what he had to do.

"I shouldn't have brought you in here," he said after another deep breath.

Then Kris turned to face her, to look her directly in the eye as he spoke, because she deserved that much.

"I'm not in a position to do this. I knew that when I stood there watching you but I could not turn away. When you confronted me, for a moment I thought... I wondered." He paused and cleared his throat.

"Please accept my apologies. It will not happen again."

He gave her a curt nod and turned to leave, all the while ignoring the inquisitive...no, the assessing look in her eyes.

"It will," she said the moment his fingers touched the doorknob. "You won't like it and I'll probably regret it, but I'm betting that it will happen, Your Highness. That's just the way life goes."

Kris walked out. He did not turn back. But he did not forget her words, not that night, nor the nights that followed.

Chapter 7

"The Ambassador's Ball is not far away. How many dresses do I have to choose from?" Malayka asked Landry as she lounged just a few feet away from the pool.

They were at the south side of the palace, outside, where an infinity pool's edge led down a steep cliff and waves from the sea crashed below. The view was stunning—the brilliant blue ocean reminded Landry of watercolors and the crisp clear powder blue of the sky with its cotton-candy-like clouds never failed to take her breath away. Even with the view, Landry preferred the inside pool near the court-yard because she didn't have to battle with the harsh rays of the Caribbean sun there.

Malayka, on the other hand, had the straps to her hot-pink bikini top pulled down as she lay with her caramel-toned skin glistening in the sun. When she was done, the woman would either have a sun-kissed complexion all over, or look like a ripe tomato.

"Peta is sending the last two you requested—they should be here next week. Since we're not able to use samples and in addition to the changes to the design you requested, they were delayed a few days. Right now there's the blue Balenciaga and the white Versace." Landry spoke from where she sat in a chair beneath an umbrella-topped table. She knew better than to add the fact that they couldn't use samples because most designer samples came in a size 4. Malayka was a 6 or an 8. Landry had made the mistake of mentioning sample sizes before and Malayka had rewarded her with a complete meltdown. Another lesson learned for Landry even though she thought the performance had been more dramatic than authentic. In her business Landry recognized the whole body shaming and desire to be as thin as possible debacle. Only, in Landry's mind, she'd always tried to instill in her clients that size did not matter; it was what was on the inside that counted. That particular conversation had fallen on deaf ears where Malayka was concerned. Still, the woman didn't have to work too hard to keep her cute curvy figure and now that she'd snagged herself a prince, Landry wondered if she would even bother at all after the nuptials.

Resisting the urge to shake her head in pity, Landry decided to focus on something else. Her tablet was propped in front of her, a glass of almost-finished mango lemonade beside it. She held her pen and scribbled notes on the pad she always brought to meetings and kept her sunglasses on, more so to keep Malayka from witnessing her rolling her eyes at the uppity tone the woman had adopted over the last couple of weeks.

Landry had already decided that when the dress arrived from Detali she would simply slip it in with the other dresses for consideration. She had no plans of telling Malayka who had designed the dress until the woman expressed how much she loved it. Landry was banking on that reaction, especially after meeting twice with Detali to look at the design. It was a totally original dress, which would immediately appeal to Malayka. A one-of-a-kind was just what the princess should be wearing. Landry was certain that's how Malayka would feel and she'd better be right or she would certainly be losing her job.

"Are you listening to me?"

Landry lifted her head as Malayka raised her voice. She did not appreciate being yelled at. This wasn't something Landry had needed to tell the people she worked with, even though some of her clients were rumored to have a diva complex. Of course, the relationship with her and her clients tended to go a lot smoother when her assistant Kelli was with her, but that wasn't possible for this trip. Malayka insisted on Landry coming alone.

"Yes," Landry replied. "You're thinking that we should have approached Eleni Verenzia about a dress. However, after the last episode where you returned four original pieces from her, she's not inclined to work with us again."

Landry said *us* but really Eleni just did not want any of her original designs worn by Malayka. Landry had warned Malayka against the unreasonable demands she'd required of the designer.

Clearly annoyed now, because she was undoubtedly hoping to chastise Landry for her lack of attention, Malayka waved her left hand, that huge chunk of gem on her ring finger catching the sunlight. Luckily, Landry had her sunglasses on so the glare didn't bother her too much. Still it was a reminder of something she'd been trying desperately to push out of her mind.

"If she wants to hold a grudge over something so trivial then so be it. I have other options," Malayka quipped.

"Yes. You do," Landry said as she exchanged an email

with Detali's daughter because the woman did not like computers herself. The dress would be ready tomorrow. Detali wanted to deliver it to the palace personally, but Landry's response had been that she would come into town to pick it up. Malayka had a spa day scheduled for tomorrow while Rafe attended to all-day meetings, which meant that Landry would have those hours to herself.

"Do you know where Cheryl is? I thought she was coming to this meeting as well. I told them that I changed my mind and now I want them here before I select my outfits. I mean, it makes perfect sense that when we talk about what I'm going to wear that my makeup artist and hair stylist be here as well. The full package has to be on point at all times," Malayka remarked as she used a peach hand towel that matched her bikini to dab at imaginary sweat on her forehead.

"I thought Cheryl and Amari would be here as well. I sent them each a text last night about the time we would be meeting," Landry said because she knew Malayka would want to know if she'd done her part. Another person may have found it hard to deal with the new Malayka, but Landry was thick-skinned in this arena. She knew the worst-case scenario where her clients were concerned and she also knew the line she'd drawn in her mind for work. And there definitely was a line. Malayka, luckily, had not crossed it just yet. So Landry continued to work without letting the woman's complaints and comments worry her.

Besides, it was too beautiful on this island to be stressed about anything or anyone. Even the prince who had gotten her all hot and bothered last week and then left her standing— unfulfilled—in the changing room. That, she definitely did not want to think about while sitting by the pool.

She'd been doing a good job at ignoring both Malayka and thoughts about the prince until a shadow approaching out of the corner of her eye caught Landry's attention. She didn't bother to turn because she knew who it was from the way her body had instantly warmed.

"There was an accident. Igor apparently lost control of the car and ran off the road down a small embankment," Kris said without preamble when both Landry and Malayka had looked up upon his arrival.

Malayka moved first, jumping up quickly, the top of her bikini moving just as fast, exposing her breasts. Kris managed to turn to face Landry just in time.

"Rafe? Oh my God, Rafe? Is he alright?" Malayka asked.

Landry had already skirted around where Kris stood to stand in front of Malayka, attempting to fix her top, he surmised.

"Tell me about Rafe. What's happened to him? You tell me right now!" Malayka demanded.

Landry faced him then, still blocking Malayka.

"Is he alright?" she asked, her eyes wide, voice just a little shaky.

Kris didn't like the way Landry sounded and he didn't know why he'd asked where she was the moment he'd returned to the palace. Ingrid had readily told him as she'd been assigned to keep an eye on Landry for him. So instead of going to his office or calling for his brother and sister, he'd come to find her.

"My father is safe," Kris replied and gritted his teeth so tight his temples throbbed.

"Oh my…oh," Malayka began and dropped down onto the lounge where she'd been seated, a hand clutching her chest. "Thank you, thank you, thank you. He's safe. Okay, so where is he? I know that Igor was driving him today."

"I thought your father's driver was Rex," Landry said.

She hadn't even looked back at Malayka, but continued to stare at him.

"Rex was ill. Some sort of stomach virus, Dr. Beaumont told us late last night. My father had a meeting at the mines this afternoon and since Rex still wasn't feeling better, he assigned Igor to drive him."

"I knew he was with Igor. That big oaf almost killed my Rafe. Where is he, Kris? You tell me right now. I have a right to know!"

She'd stood again and this time had pushed past Landry until she was standing directly in Kris's face. He liked it better when she was a distance away.

"My father and Jose Realto, the mine supervisor, have been friends for a very long time. Two days ago Jose became a grandfather for the first time. He and his wife, Juanita, invited my father to a celebratory dinner. And that's why my father was *not* in the car when Igor drove off the road."

"Then where the hell is he?"

She was much shorter than Kris's tall frame. Her wavy hair had been pulled back from her face and she wore large round-framed sunglasses that looked too big for her small stature. And she was loud. This wasn't the first time he'd witnessed this and Kris knew it wouldn't be the last. Still, this was the woman his father loved, the one that would soon be the princess of this island. He almost flinched at the thought.

"Maybe you should tell her so she can go see him," Landry said, reminding him that she was still there and that he'd much prefer talking to her.

Looking over Malayka's shoulder Kris found surprising relief at seeing Landry staring at him, her sunglasses now removed as she clenched them in one hand.

"He's in the infirmary, on the lower level of the palace

with Dr. Beaumont. Igor is down there being treated. They believe he has a concussion and a broken arm, but other than that he will recover."

"Well, I'm certainly glad he will recover since he's the one who drove off the damn road!" Malayka continued, before pushing past Kris this time and heading toward the house.

Kris rubbed a hand down the back of his head and let out rugged sigh.

"He's okay," he heard Landry say. "That's good that your father was not injured and Igor will recover."

He nodded, words clogging his throat at the moment. He didn't know which words and that was a problem. There should be no problem speaking. He should know exactly what to say to everyone, at all times.

She touched his arm and Kris looked at her and nodded.

"Alright, well that's a good thing," she continued. "He's safe and he's unharmed. So why don't you just take a deep breath and let that sink in."

What was she talking about?

Kris couldn't answer that question either because he was busy doing as she'd suggested.

"The call came just as I was leaving our attorney's office. I drove straight to the scene because the officer told me my father was not in the car. The car is totaled—it's a miracle that Igor is even alive," he told her.

She continued touching his arm, this time moving her hand up and down in a motion that should not be so soothing. Yet, it was.

"They're going to do a complete investigation and keep me abreast of everything." He nodded again. "So that's it. The prince is fine. Igor is fine."

"But you're not," she said quietly.

Kris did not respond for what seemed like endless moments.

"Have you ever had a normal dinner, Your Highness?"

"Stop calling me that," was his immediate reply. It was in the wrong tone, but he was agitated and frustrated, though, none of that was her fault. Still, she quickly moved her hand from his arm.

"My name is Kristian," he told her after forcing himself to calm. "You can call me Kris."

She looked like she might actually argue with him, but instead gave a slight hunch of her shoulders and then continued.

"Have you ever had a fully loaded pizza and a beer for dinner, Kris?" she asked.

Why was she talking about food? Was she asking him on a date?

While he was coming up with more questions instead of answering her, she continued.

"I'm sure you've never been asked on a date," she continued. "But I don't count this as a *real* date. You need to unwind after this emotional jolt. I know, because when my father fell off a ladder as he tried to change some filter in the church basement, I was hysterical. For the twenty minutes that the doctors thought he might need a hip replacement, I was a nervous nutcase. Those were my brother's words, not my own assessment, by the way."

Yellow was her color, Kris thought absently as he continued to watch her talk. The white pants she wore were fitting every curve of her hips and bottom, but it was the off-the-shoulder yellow top that made her eyes seem brighter, her cheeks just a little higher. Yes, he liked her in that color.

"But once the doctors said he was going to be alright without surgery," she continued, as if she had no idea he was assessing every tiny nuance of her. "I was so relieved I returned to my condo and ordered a whole pizza with all the toppings and grabbed a six-pack of beer. I'd never been a beer drinker before but I felt like I needed something extra that night. I only drank one—gave the other five to my brother the next morning—but the pizza, I completely devoured it."

She gave the smallest smile just as she reached out to touch his arm again. Why did her touch alone calm him in a way that no amount of slow breathing or confirmations from Rafe had been able to do?

"I think it can help you too," Landry finished with a tilt of her head as she looked up at him.

"It might," Kris said. "But I'm guessing that having you with me might be the bigger consolation."

He said it. He meant it. And it was done.

After a complete security check of the car and an extra mechanical check by Tajeo, Kristian and Landry were seated in the backseat headed to a trattoria located on the outskirts of the town.

"I've had pepperoni pizza before. Sam likes it with extra cheese. When she was young and had tea parties, she always had pizza to go along with it. Roland and I weren't invited to the parties, but we snuck into the kitchen and stole slices of pizza before Ingrid had a chance to put them on a platter the way Sam had requested."

Kris had no idea why he'd told her that.

No, that was wrong. He knew why he'd told her, just like he knew why he'd sought her out instead of any of the members of his family. He might not like the answer, but he was certain he now knew for sure.

"My sister, Paula, likes pepperoni too. We can get the meat lovers' pizza with extra cheese if you prefer," she offered.

They were only a couple feet apart. Close enough for him to reach out and take her hand, to have something to hold on to for just a moment. He needed that, but he refrained.

"No. This was your idea so I'm going to try everything you suggest. The loaded pizza with a beer," he answered and then looked over to her.

She was nodding, a smile on her face. "You're gonna love it," she told him.

Kris managed to smile in return as he wondered, what if? His thoughts circled back to why he'd sought her out today, why he'd wanted to see her and only her during this emotional time. Could he possibly? No. He wasn't falling for her. He couldn't be.

"You're picking most of the toppings off your pizza," Kris told her, unable to hide the amusement from his tone.

With all the wonderful places to eat with his favored Caribbean cuisine, Kris found himself quite comfortable seated at the center table in the trattoria. Tajeo had gone in ahead of Kris to let the owners know that he was there. After a ten-minute wait while two patrons finished their meal, settled with the waiter and walked out, Kris stepped out of the car. He waved Tajeo off when he reached to open the door for Landry. Kris opened it himself and offered her his hand. She took it, smiling up at him as she climbed out of the backseat.

"So gallant," she said. "A girl can certainly get used to this treatment."

"A woman should always be treated with the utmost care and respect," he told her as he continued to hold her hand in his.

She did not respond to that, which was a surprise since she usually had a response to everything.

Once inside, they were seated, and Landry enthusiastically placed their order. Tajeo had locked the front door himself and stood there while the staff waited on them only.

"I don't really like the sausage," she admitted in reply to his statement about the pizza. "Or the black olives."

Kris finished chewing the last bite of his second slice. "Then why order a pizza with everything on it?"

"Because it sounds bold and decisive. Like, *I dare you to call me a picky eater*," she told him and took a bite of her second slice that now only had pepperoni, ham, red onions and green peppers.

Kris was allergic to mushrooms so they'd requested a pizza without them.

"You didn't like people calling you names?" he asked.

She shook her head and used her napkin to wipe her mouth before she spoke. "I didn't like my brothers doing anything they wanted and assuming that I couldn't. So whatever they did, I did it too. Sometimes I did it better. But I could not eat raw onions on a hot dog with ketchup. The smell was revolting. The one time I tried, I ended up with my face in the toilet. The next time my mother cooked hot dogs, my brother Geoffrey said I couldn't have any because I was a picky eater. They called me that every time we sat down for a meal for the next month."

Kris couldn't help but smile at that story because it reminded him a lot of how Roland used to treat Sam. "You do know that it's a brother's job to taunt his sister. Is Geoffrey older than you?"

"Yes, I know that's a brother's job. I also knew how to get back at them, as a sister. I let the air out of the tires on all of their bikes," she replied triumphantly. "Four brothers older than me and a younger sister. My parents always wanted a big family."

"Sounds like you had some interesting times," Kris said as he reached for another slice.

He liked the pizza. The beer was just okay. He had a better selection back at the palace, but he would not think of offending the owners by not emptying his glass. Kris was very aware of how nervous the owner looked as he directed his staff to wait on him and Landry. It wasn't every day that the crown prince brought a date to this little spot. In fact, this had never happened before.

"Did you have interesting times when you were a kid?" she asked before taking another bite.

Kris picked up his napkin and wiped his fingers before sitting back in his seat. He contemplated the question, wondering just how he should answer. How much should he tell? How much was too much?

"Did you taunt your sister and beat up your little brother?" she continued with a chuckle. "I cannot imagine you doing either, but I could be wrong."

She wasn't wrong. Not entirely.

"Sam hates spiders," Kris began, the memory startlingly fresh in his mind. "One day when my father was away and I had some time to myself, I spent the entire day walking the property, going into the wooded area just beyond the palace walls. I collected a jar full of spiders." He shrugged.

"I'm not sure I was thinking of what I'd do with them at the time, but when I returned to the house Sam was having one of her dinner parties. She was always hosting a party in the palace."

"She had to entertain herself," Landry offered.

"I guess so. For this one party she wanted Roland and I to attend and she asked us to dress up. I was tired of dressing up. I wanted to eat dinner in my shorts and T-shirt and to keep on the tennis shoes I was wearing even if they were covered in dirt.

"Ingrid insisted that I change. *Let's make your sister happy today*, she'd said. I didn't want to make anyone happy that day. I wanted to make myself happy." Kris lifted his glass and took a sip of the second beer the manager had quietly brought to him.

"I knew that my mother would not like it if she found out that I'd disobeyed Ingrid. And my father would totally lose it if he found out that I'd attended a dinner dressed in shorts and a T-shirt. So I changed and I went down to the main dining room, which had been decorated in pink-and-yellow ribbons. Dolls had been set in each of the chairs at the table except the ones left empty for me and Roland. I sat down and I ate the ridiculous pink cake and sipped the lemonade. Then, when Ingrid walked into the kitchen and Sam was up tending to one of her dolls, I took the jar that I'd slipped into the pocket of my suit jacket and set it in Sam's chair. I removed the lid and then I returned to my seat. I'd just finished my lemonade when Sam screamed.

"There was complete chaos then as you can imagine everyone came running to see what was wrong with the princess. I stood stoically then and put each of the spiders back into the jar. I was punished for the duration of the evening," he finished.

She propped her elbows on the table and watched him intently as he spoke, as if she was thoroughly amused.

"What did you do during your punishment?"

"I sat on my bed and stared at that jar of spiders, giggling every few minutes at the look on Sam's face when she saw them. In the morning I felt bad and went to Sam's room before breakfast to apologize to her. She hit me with her pillow and then made me sit through a private tea party with her special dolls."

"But you were okay with that because you got the chance to do something fun," Landry said thoughtfully.

"You didn't have much time for fun growing up, I suspect. Just like you don't now."

He sat up straighter then, feeling as if too many eyes were on him and he wasn't at his best, or rather his guard had been lowered, when it shouldn't have been.

Clearing his throat, Kris looked at her directly. "I have a duty. The rest is secondary."

In the next moments he gave a nod of his head and the staff were moving to clear the table. He'd asked if she wanted the rest of the pizza and when she'd nodded, he instructed the staff to box it and another one to go.

"Are we returning to the palace?" she asked when he'd stood and waited for her to join him.

Kris looked at her then. He recalled the way her cheeks lifted when she smiled and the sound of her voice as she laughed. He'd watched her lick her lips after each bite of her pizza and frown over the bitter taste of the beer. She'd listened to his story with complete attentiveness and had hit the nail squarely on the head with her assessment of why that memory meant so much to him. She was getting to him; he knew it. He didn't like it, but he couldn't deny it.

"No. Not yet," Kris told her.

Landry giggled as she walked barefoot along the shoreline. Night had fallen, only slithers of moonlight bouncing along the water's edge.

She had no idea when was the last time she'd giggled. Probably never. Landry had always been on a mission to prove to her older brothers that she was just as strong as them, just as resilient as anyone else. She was a girl, but she was not a ninny. How many times had she told them that? She'd lost count.

Yet when she'd tripped over her own stupid feet and almost fell into the rolling tide, Kris had easily wrapped an arm around her waist, saving her from inevitable embarrassment. His grip had been strong and her feet had left the ground almost immediately. It wasn't necessary, but he'd swung her around then, so that the cooler evening breeze brushed over her cheeks and lifted the ends of her hair.

He'd wrapped both his arms around her and held her tight to his chest and as she'd let her head fall back and giggled, he'd chuckled too.

She stared at him as he slowly let her slide down until her feet once again touched the sand. He seemed darker out here, they both did, Landry supposed. But there was something else. A shield had been lowered. She could see it in the lift of his lips and the light in his eyes.

"What? Why are you staring at me like that?" he asked, his hands slipping away from her arms.

"You're different," she told him. "Relaxed."

He immediately stopped smiling. "I'm on the beach and it's getting dark," he replied.

"Are you afraid of the dark?" she asked as she stepped closer to him.

She liked being close to him. Liked it way too much. She'd had one beer in comparison to his two, still Landry felt like it must be going to her head.

"I'm not," he replied.

Landry nodded. "You're not afraid of anything, are you, Kristian? Not afraid of anything, can complete any task, handle any catastrophe. You're all that, but still, right here and now, you're still different."

He sighed then and looked away.

"You don't have to say anything. I just mentioned it," she told him. "I know I can be pushy sometimes, but I'm really not trying to be."

When he didn't respond Landry wondered how she was going to get out of this uncomfortable situation she'd just created. Why couldn't she have just kept her mouth shut and continued with the spinning and giggling?

"You don't treat me like everyone else," he said quietly as he took a few steps back from her and then turned to face the ocean.

"You're not like anyone else I've ever met," she admitted, her voice almost as quiet as his.

The waves seemed much louder then; the wind and every little thing around them seemed bigger, more pronounced than just a few seconds ago. She lifted her hands to push her hair back behind her ears while she tried to figure out why.

"Because I'm a prince?"

Landry shook her head. "And because you're much more complicated than I first realized. There's more in there, isn't there? You walk so tall and hold your head so high. You rule and you organize. But do you live?"

She'd had this very same thought since the days that followed their tryst in the changing room. When Kris had left her alone after apologizing and telling her that it—*they*— would not happen again, she'd told him that it would. Later that night she'd thought that perhaps she should not have said that. Kristian appeared to be a decisive man, something Landry thought came with his title and upbringing. Then she'd dreamt of him, of them making love beneath the warm Caribbean sun. He was smiling in that dream, touching her and enjoying her as she had enjoyed him. In the morning she'd tried to forget the dream but that hadn't worked and eventually her thoughts had turned to the man that would forego physical pleasure for the sake of duty.

He stood with his legs spread slightly apart. Before they'd climbed out of the car to enter the restaurant she'd convinced him to remove his suit jacket by saying, *It feels*

like it's near one hundred degrees out there. You're mak-
ing me hot just looking at you all buttoned up in that suit.

Surprisingly, he'd only given her an amused look before
removing his jacket. A part of Landry hadn't been sure
whether he would simply direct his driver to take them
back to the palace or argue his position with her. The silent acquiescence had caused a different type of trepida-
tion in her where the prince was concerned.

Now, he'd even slackened the blue-gray tie he wore so
that it hung loosely around his open shirt collar. He still
looked out to the water, his hands calmly at his sides.

"I live the life I was meant to live," he responded to
the question Landry had nearly forgotten as she'd been so
caught up in staring at him.

"Me too," she said, looking out to the water as well.
"You ever wonder if there's more though?"

Again, Kristian didn't answer right away. That was fine
because Landry figured her mouth had once again gotten
her into a strained situation. She now found herself thinking about her job and her life back home and if that was
all she was ever going to have.

"My mother always wanted more," Kristian commented
after a while. "She was always bursting with energy and
enthusiasm. I could look into her eyes every day and see a
new plan for some outing or event at the palace. Something
she wanted to do with children or to save the environment.
Then, just hours later when I was finished with whatever
my father had on my schedule for the day, I'd see her and
Sam playing in Sam's bedroom. There was so much pink
in there, dolls and doll clothes, a huge doll house that had
enough furniture for a human family to reside in it. Her
voice was animated and Sam loved it. One day when I
asked her how she managed to do all those things, she said
simply, *I love my life and I have love in my life.*"

Landry nodded because she knew exactly what his mother had been trying to tell him. Not that this was the way she'd wanted this little outing with Kristian to go. She'd only intended to take his mind off the accident. And she definitely did not want to talk about falling in love and all the ties and rules that went with that.

She walked farther into the water, not really caring that the hems of her capri pants were now getting wet. When she decided she was far enough and Kristian had not said another word, she turned and began kicking water in his direction.

"I'll bet your mother loved this water," she said. "I've been swimming in the pool, but yesterday I finally had a chance to get down to the beach and it's fantastic!"

He looked like he had when she'd asked him to take off his suit jacket and Landry figured she'd be the only one riding back to the palace with wet clothes on, until Kristian surprised her yet again. He didn't rush over and dunk her beneath the water, which is exactly what her brothers would have done. Instead, he approached her, his own pants getting just as wet as hers, and cupped her face in his hands.

Needless to say, Landry immediately stopped kicking water. She may have actually stopped breathing as Kristian's face was suddenly very close to hers. So close her lips parted involuntarily in anticipation.

"You're not supposed to be here," he said, his voice strained. "This is not supposed to happen."

Landry didn't know how to respond to that. What should she say? Or should she maybe just leave? Wade her way out of the water and back to the car that was waiting for them on the bank a short distance away. That would not be a very dignified exit, but it might put a stop to the struggle she heard so clearly in his voice.

Of course that's not what she did because that would have been the easiest and most sensible thing to do. For Landry, there really was no choice.

She moved in closer, eliminating that small breath of space between them and touched his lips with hers. She did not go softly either. It was all or nothing at this point, she figured. Hell, she'd told the prince to take off his jacket, why not go all the way and kiss him beneath the moonlight too?

Chapter 8

Kris kicked the door to his private rooms closed and reached back to make sure the lock clicked into place. He still had an arm around Landry's waist because he hadn't been able to stop touching her the entire ride back to the palace.

The kiss in the water had unleashed something inside him, something he was more than tired of holding back. When they'd finally taken a break for air, Kris hadn't hesitated when he scooped Landry up in his arms and carried her back to the car. She ran her fingers along the line of his jaw as he held her, staring up at him as if she knew exactly what he was thinking. He'd thought the same about her question about him really living his life. How could she have known the one question that haunted him every day?

He'd told her this wasn't supposed to happen, that she wasn't supposed to be here, but Kris was beginning to think that was all wrong.

Tajeo had stood stoically with the back door of the car open and Kris had gently set Landry inside. On the ride back, Kris had pulled her close, his arm locked around her shoulder while he stared forward. She laid her head on his shoulder and they rode in silence, consumed by their thoughts.

He wondered if she knew that his thoughts were totally focused on getting her naked and beneath him in the shortest amount of time possible?

At the palace, Kris walked them through the back door and stepped onto an elevator that the staff normally used. He guided her down the lengthy hallway to his rooms and now could only stare down into her eyes.

"If you don't want this I need you to say so right now," he said, the words tight in his throat, need burning in his gut.

He hadn't bothered to turn on any lights, but several windows were free of the blinds he usually activated at night, so the moonlight spilled in, casting a sensual hue throughout the area.

"I want this," was her simple reply.

Why did everything seem that way with her? It had been so easy for him to watch her night after night as she swam and even easier to lead her into that changing room with him. Even tonight, going to have dinner with her— pizza, of all things—had seemed so natural and necessary at the same time.

When her hand flattened on his chest, Kris touched her cheek once more, moving until he could kiss her again. Their tongues twined softly together, mixing in a gentle prequel to what he knew was going to be a long night.

She moaned softly as he kissed the line of her jaw, down to her neck. Her fingers gripped his arms as his tongue touched the smooth skin of her shoulder. Since he'd approached her at the pool earlier, Kris had been enamored by the line of her shoulders, now bared with the design of her blouse. The contrast between her complexion and the bright tone of the shirt was nothing short of alluring. While his hand cupped one shoulder, his fingers moving slowly over her soft skin, his tongue stroked over the other, gentle kisses turning quickly into suckling, nipping.

"Kristian." She whispered his name as she leaned into him.

He'd asked her to call him Kris. She hadn't. Not one time. He groaned and her hands moved until she was cupping the back of his head.

Desperate to see and taste more, Kris pushed the rim of her shirt until she let her arms fall to her sides and he could maneuver the blouse until it was bunched at her waist. She wore a strapless bra that barely contained the heavy mounds of her breasts. With movements so slow they were almost painful, Kris unhooked that bra and watched it fall to the floor. Using the back of his fingers he rubbed over both nipples until they were hard and enticing. Could they…or she, be more tempting than he'd already found her to be? He didn't think so.

"I won't break," she told him, her tone a breathy whisper.

His gaze found hers quickly and he replied, "I'm afraid I will."

She touched his wrists then, bringing her fingers down until they were covering his on her chest. She squeezed his hands, which resulted in him squeezing her breasts. She gasped; her tongue slipped out to stroke her lips. He squeezed again on his own accord this time, watching intently as passion filled her eyes.

"More," she encouraged him and Kris felt as if the heat in this room might suffocate him.

She felt wonderful in his hands, more so than anything Kris had ever touched before. He knew the second his name fell from her lips again that he needed more as well. Bending slightly, he replaced one hand on her breast with his tongue on her nipple. Stroking it slowly, loving the pebble-hard feel of her flesh against his tongue. Opening his mouth he sucked deep, pulling as much of her into his mouth as he could, inhaling and exhaling to keep himself upright and focused. Squeezing and sucking, her hands tight on the back of his head, her voice telling him, "Yes. More. Please, Kristian," crashed through his system like a torrential storm.

Kris picked her up then, cradling her in his arms as he bent down to take her mouth once more. She hugged him close, meeting the quick and hungry licks of his tongue with mounting fervor of her own. When his feet bumped the platform of his bed, he reluctantly pulled his lips away from hers; their breaths quickened as he rested his forehead against hers for a few seconds.

He placed her gently on his bed, bending immediately to remove the sandals from her feet. There was still a bit of sand there, on her toes, even though she'd wiped furiously with the towel Tajeo had provided for them when they'd returned from the beach. Kris brushed away the tiny sparkles, loving the twinkle of the fiery red polish on her toenails. Next, he reached up to undo the snap of her pants. She was watching him, her gaze intent on every movement of his fingers. Kris found that very arousing and continued.

She lifted her hips slightly off the bed so that he could pull her pants down her legs. His fingers brushed over her thighs and when her pants were completely removed and lying on the floor somewhere behind him, he returned his hands there. Kneading the soft skin, loving the feel of pliant limbs beneath his palms. He pressed gently against her inner thighs and sighed with pleasure as she spread her legs farther for him. Again, his fingers moved over her skin, his pulse quickening as he watched his lighter-toned skin against hers. When his thumbs scraped the material of her panties, Kris had to pause. He closed his eyes, moving his fingers over the puffiness of her mound, and sucked in a deep breath. Closer, his mind roared. He had to get closer.

The shirt came next and Kris heard the distinct tear of material as he'd opted to pull that down her legs as well. He'd have to buy her a new one. A dozen more of this same design, in bright, vibrant colors that would make her skin glow and her smile seem magical.

She was naked now…no, she still wore white panties. The ones that came up high on her waist and were made of what felt like a simple cotton. They should have been too demure to be sexy, too plain to be memorable, but Kris knew he'd never forget them. Not the way they both highlighted and hid the part of her that he ached to see most.

When he reached down to remove them, she shocked him by pushing his hands away.

"Let me," she said, her gaze trained on his as she hooked her thumbs beneath the rim of her panties and pushed them down slowly.

Inch by delicious inch she was bared to him and Kris's mouth watered with anticipation. He wanted to taste and touch, to look and explore, to feel and be felt, all at once.

Moving close to the edge of the bed she reached up and worked the buttons on his shirt until she was able to push it free of his arms. His undershirt came next as Kris found himself watching her fingers in the same way that she'd previously watched his. Her hands were much smaller than his, but still they moved deftly over his body leaving his skin to tingle with warmth as she did so.

They were both naked now. Him standing in front of her, looking down at the dark circles of her nipples, and her looking at him. His chest, his waist, his thighs, his arousal. She perused every part of him, making Kris feel not only naked, but vulnerable to her as well. It wasn't a feeling he was used to, not one that he was certain he knew how to handle, but that was okay. Or at least that's what she'd told him.

"Condoms," she whispered.

"Huh?" he asked, his mind still flip-flopping between being so aroused it was near painful and being afraid that even with his title, he may somehow be lacking to her.

She smiled, running a finger along his lower abs. "Where are your condoms?"

Kris smiled in return as reality slapped him soundly in the face. He moved away from her—even though her touch had been doing something else to him, something sinfully delicious—and retrieved a wooden box from his nightstand drawer. He kept it full of condoms even though he'd never brought a woman there. After setting the box on the nightstand and removing one, he walked to her and on impulse gave her the foil packet.

She opened it immediately and reached for him. Kris groaned inwardly as he stepped closer to her, his body tense with need as he watched her fingers close around him. She stroked him once, twice, and the last edges of his control slipped. Kris sighed and closed his eyes.

Again she stroked him, this time touching his sac lightly. It was enough to have him cursing and gritting his teeth as she did it again and again, until he was thrusting in her hand like a horny teenager about to find his release.

"Enough!" Kris finally managed. His heart was pounding so hard he wasn't sure it was healthy.

She slid the condom on him then and moved back on the

bed when she was finished. When he thought she would hold her arms out and welcome him, she did not. Instead she leaned back on her elbows, with her legs partially spread and waited.

"If you don't want this, I need you to say so right now," she said to him, repeating what he'd asked of her not too long ago.

"I want it," he said without preamble. "Damn it all to hell, but I want it."

Relief rippled through Landry like waves at the ocean. She didn't speak, or show it in any way—at least she hoped she hadn't—but her legs trembled as he touched them. She licked her bottom lip and tried to hold his gaze as he moved over her. That was a task since she'd never been more aroused by a man touching her thighs than she was with him. There was just something about his strong, aristocratic fingers clutching her skin. It made her feel sexier than she'd ever imagined, especially since her thighs and her stomach had always been the parts of her body Landry hated most.

No, she wasn't a slim girl by the world's standards, nor was she technically a thick girl. Somewhere in between was where she'd found herself in her senior year of high school, fluctuating between a size twelve and fourteen. She had a butt and thighs and her waist could use a good cincher, or maybe liposuction, even though she'd never seriously considered either. Now, even though she purchased more size twelves and fit them all perfectly, Landry still loved her curves and dressed to fit her confident and vivacious personality, nothing more and nothing less.

Still, every woman had insecurities about their body, she surmised. Even her smallest client who wore a size two hated her breasts because she thought they were too small. It was a never-ending cycle for women and Landry gave it the time it required. No less than seconds each day.

Tonight, she was in heaven as Kris's gaze was nothing but appreciative of every part of her body. He'd held her D cup breasts in his palms as if he were holding something as precious as the finest china. Then he'd suckled them like he was tasting the best wine ever. But it was when he touched her thighs, when his fingers were on the inside, moving close to her center that she'd known she was done. It was over, whatever resistance there might be in her mind, her body was down for this and whatever else was about to come.

Still, she'd needed the verbal acquiescence, just as he had moments ago.

His fingers were past her thighs now, parting her folds to touch the moistness he'd evoked. Landry sucked in a breath, then let it out slowly as he moved a finger up and down, stirring her juices until she wanted to scream with excitement.

"I wanted to go slow," he said, his voice husky and strained. "We should. I mean, it's the first time, so it should be memorable and…"

"Please," Landry said, cutting him off.

She lay back on the bed and spread her legs wider. Her body humming with desire as his finger continued to move over her tender flesh. She lifted her hips in an effort to guide him.

"Now," she finally whispered. "Right. Now."

He did not hesitate, but sank a finger, plus another, inside her. Landry grabbed the smooth, cool comforter beneath her and resisted the urge to call out. He pumped his fingers in and out of her until she was squirming beneath him.

"Now," he whispered. "Right. Now."

He was over her in seconds, the thick tip of his erection replacing his fingers, stretching her in a move that was so wonderful she could do nothing but sigh. He pumped easily, pressing into her in excruciatingly slow movements.

If there was such a thing as perfection Landry thought this was definitely it. He was filling her. It was tight and warm and so good, her arms trembled as she lifted them to wrap around his shoulders when he leaned forward. He came down on his elbows that he'd planted on either side of her head. His face was close to hers, his body deeply embedded inside hers.

Landry opened her eyes to see him staring down at her. The sadness she'd seen earlier when he'd been talking about his mother had been clouded over by desire. He desired her. The Caribbean prince desired the American stylist. She couldn't believe it and yet, instinctively, Landry felt like it meant so much more. He continued to watch her as he moved. When she lifted her legs, locking them behind his back, he leaned in closer to kiss her lips and Landry knew in that instant, that this was definitely more.

It was just before dawn when Landry managed to move unnoticed from beneath Kris's arm and slip out of his bed. Collecting her clothes wasn't easy, but she'd managed without tripping over anything.

Sometime during the night his blinds had closed partially so that the light that came with a burgeoning sunrise now filtered into the space. It was a very large space, and this was just the bedroom portion. She remembered walking into a full-fledged living room last night and entering through the double doors of his massive room. His bed was huge, sitting back against a side wall of the room on a two-foot-high platform. The bed faced a wall of windows that Landry took a couple of seconds to stand closer to.

This view was phenomenal with a breathtaking drop down the cliffs to where the water crashed and rolled against the rocks. She had more of a beach view in her room, but this right here was simply spectacular. Too bad she did not have time to dawdle. She needed to be out of there before anyone in the house awakened to see her leaving this room. And of course, before Kristian awoke.

Tiptoeing out into the living room where she dressed quickly, Landry barely looked around at the leather furniture and plush rugs. There was a huge desk and chair, a television on another wall, a fireplace and bookshelves. That gave her pause as she wondered what type of books a man like Kristian read. She didn't stay to find out, but moved faster until she made it to the door that she knew would take her out into the hallway. The door had been locked even though she had no recollection of Kristian doing so when they'd come in last night. She unlocked it and slipped slowly out into the hallway.

It was a long walk to her room, so Landry decided to run. Yes, she held her shoes in her hand and ran all the way to her room, not stopping until she was safe behind the door. Then she breathed a sigh of relief about two seconds before a sound scared the crap out of her.

Chapter 9

"You wanna tell me what you think you're doing?"

Kris stopped the moment he walked out of his bedroom to see Roland leaning against the wall, arms folded, face frowning.

"I'd like an answer to that question as well," Sam chimed in from where she sat in one of the reclining chairs in the center of his living room.

A unified attack, Kris thought as he straightened his tie and walked past the both of them, heading toward the minibar in the corner. "Good morning to you both," he muttered.

"It almost wasn't a good morning," Roland continued. "When were you going to tell us that you didn't think Igor's running off the road was an accident?"

"I'm still waiting for a call from my brother to tell me that the car my father was supposed to be riding in was in an accident. But not to worry because my father is safe and sound," Sam added.

If he were actively paying attention to them Kris's neck would have been sore from volleying back and forth between his brother and sister. As it stood, he wanted his usual cup of steaming-hot black coffee, before he actually began talking to either of them.

He was wearing a blue suit today, the usual white shirt and a pink-and-blue tie. He had yet to button his jacket, but knew that the creases in his pants were perfect and the light starch order on his shirt had been well done. He looked the part of the ambitious prince ready for the workday, even if, on the inside, he didn't feel like it.

His coffee—which was already in the pot awaiting him as per the automatic setting—was hot and bitter. It had almost spilled down the front of his pristine white shirt when his brother yelled.

"Dammit, Kris! Don't stand there with your stoic expression and just ignore us!" Roland had pushed away from the wall and now stood beside the chair where Sam sat.

"First," Kris spoke as he set his cup on the counter. "It's too early in the morning for yelling. And furthermore, it's not necessary. I hear both of your complaints and I apologize."

He'd looked up at them. "I should have called you yesterday to tell you about Dad. By the time I returned to the palace he was already in the infirmary with Dr. Beaumont. I checked on him and on Igor and then I went straight to the garage to check on the maintenance reports for the cars. The police wanted a copy, but I wanted to read them first."

Roland nodded. "You wanted to see them so you could deal with whatever was on them. Just like you talked to the police and you talked to Dad. What about us, Kris? When were you going to talk to us?"

"When did you get back in town, Roland?" Kris asked as he came to stand a few feet away from his brother.

"Because the last time I checked…oh no, wait a minute, I usually can't check on you because you don't have enough consideration to put all your globe-trotting trips on the joint calendar."

"Don't do that," Roland snapped back. "Don't try to make this about me, when we're talking about you trying to control everything."

"So you want to talk about me doing my job now? Since when did that interest you at all?" Kris countered. He was beginning to become irritated with being questioned by someone who rarely ever wanted to hear any palace business at all.

"That's enough, you two," Sam interjected. "I think what he's trying to say, Kris, is that you should have kept us in the loop."

Kris turned and was about to respond but Sam lifted a hand to stop him.

"You didn't and you have your reasons, but we're a part of this family too. If you think there was some type of sabotage afoot, we have a right to know."

Kris took another sip of his coffee. He knew they were right. He should have told them, but he hadn't. After seeing his father and speaking to the police all Kris had wanted to do was find Landry. When he had, nothing else seemed to matter. His father was safe and he planned to deal with whatever had happened out there on that road at another time. Landry was with him and he'd focused his attention on her, something he'd never done before.

"You're right and I apologize," he said slowly. That too was something he hadn't done much of in the past.

Weary after the last couple of hours and with a headache brewing, Kris took a seat on the black Biltmore Chesterfield leather couch and set his cup on the side table.

"The brakes were tampered with. The car was never

meant to stop. That's what the cops said. Igor's got a bump on his head the size of an egg and says Rex is the only one with keys to the car. The extra set stays in a lockbox in Rex's office. The car is always parked right outside of Rex's room door, not in the garage. Rex corroborated all of this and said he gave Igor the keys yesterday morning when he came to his room."

"Why aren't all the keys kept in the garage with the others?" Sam asked.

"Because Rex likes to be ready whenever Dad calls," Roland answered. "He doesn't like taking the time to get to the garage and risk the car being blocked in by another one. He's the supervisor so he can make that call."

Sam shook her head. "All the cars are the same. What difference does it make which one he uses?"

Kris looked at Roland, unable to hide his surprise that his brother knew that much about their drivers.

"Dad likes his car. He picked it out and then ordered the fleet," Kris told Sam.

"And we all know that whatever Prince Rafferty wants, he gets," Roland continued, the light tone failing so that he still sounded irritated.

His brother let out a breath and shook his head. "So if somebody messed with that car in particular, there's a good chance they knew it was Dad's car."

"You're saying someone snuck onto the palace grounds just to tamper with the brakes on Dad's car?" Sam asked, clearly not believing what she was hearing.

"It seems that way," Kris stated. "But the palace gates are locked tighter than any prison system I know of. It's almost impossible for anyone who doesn't belong here to get in."

"So that means the person that messed with Dad's car

belongs here, or at least she acts as if she does," Roland added.

A hush fell over the room.

"You're saying that Malayka tried to kill Dad?" Sam shook her head again. "I don't believe that."

"And I don't trust her," Roland stated. "She's an opportunist of the highest quality. I did some checking into her background—"

"I already ran a background check on her," Kris interrupted.

"That was a legal check, I'm sure," Roland told them. "I, on the other hand, am not compelled to use the same approved channels as you are for a thorough search into a person's background."

"What did you find?" Sam asked before Kris could question his brother further.

"I found," Roland started then paused to fold his arms over his chest and look directly at Kris, "that there is no record of Malayka Sampson living in Beverly Hills before two years ago."

"Her birth certificate says she was born in Tallahassee, Florida. She graduated from high school there and then moved," Kris stated, recalling what the report he'd had rushed to him on Malayka had said.

Roland nodded. "Moved where? She's thirty-seven years old. Where has she been since she was seventeen? My guy can find anybody, anywhere, at any time. He has access to the United States' top security networks—FBI and CIA. He also has contacts in the division formerly known as the KGB. He knows everything there is to know and then some. So why can't he find anything on her?"

Kris didn't have an answer to that question. He didn't like that realization.

"Dad was satisfied with the records from Florida," Kris told them.

Sam sat back and ran her fingers through her hair. "He told me that she was from Florida and traveled for years after she graduated with a cheerleading squad. He said she ended up living in Paris for some time, modeling and writing a book. She just returned to the States two years ago."

Roland nodded. Kris frowned.

"Does that sound strange to anyone but me?" Roland asked.

"Yes," Kris answered. He'd heard that same story from his father, after he'd shared the private investigator's report with him. Rafe hadn't seemed fazed by Kris's questions, so he'd stopped asking them. He hadn't, however, stopped wondering.

"Can your guy dig deeper?" he asked Roland. "If we can get the exact name of the cheerleading squad and trace where they were over the years, maybe get Malayka to tell us exactly where she lived in Paris, maybe we can get more information."

"That's just it," Roland told them. "He can get information on anyone, providing that person actually exists. I don't think Malayka Sampson does."

"You mean she's using a fake name?" Sam asked.

"Wait a minute," Kris interrupted. "Let's just take a second to be really clear about what we're saying."

He took a deep breath and let it out slowly. "Dad is planning to marry this woman. She's soon to become the princess of this island. She will be the second-highest ruling party in this palace. That's a lot of power."

"A lot of power," Roland conceded.

"She definitely likes power," Sam added.

Kris knew his duty. He knew he was expected to not only lead the citizens on this island, but also everyone in this palace. His mother had always told him to look after Roland and Sam, that she trusted him to do what was necessary for them throughout their lives. Vivienne trusted him. Kris tried hard to feel as if he'd earned that trust, even when he knew deep down that he hadn't. Still, it was on him, this conversation, this moment, and what the three of them did or said from this moment on, was solely on him.

"Nobody will say a word about this new investigation. It's between the three of us. And you tell your man I want this done pronto. No matter how much it costs I want to know who she is, where she's from and why the hell she's on this island."

Roland nodded his approval, his hands falling to his sides as he reached into his pocket for his cell phone.

"Sam, you find out what you can from Malayka herself. I know you don't like her but she's more likely to let something slip to a woman, than to me or Roland. I want to know everything she does. Everything her staff is doing. The hair stylist, the makeup artist, and—" Kris paused and gritted his teeth. "The stylist. I want to know their every move."

Landry breathed a sigh of relief and slapped a hand to her chest as she flattened her back against the door and saw that the sound was her cell phone, vibrating across the coffee table. She'd left it there yesterday when she'd gone to the pool to meet with Malayka. After talking to Kelli for an hour about how business was going back in Los Angeles, it needed to be charged. Her plan had been to return to her room to shower and dress for dinner as soon as the meeting was finished, so Landry hadn't been afraid of missing anything important.

Apparently, since the sun was now peeking through the open blinds in the bedroom casting hazy rays of light into the sitting area where she stood, her plans for last night had changed and now she had missed something.

Heading over to the table, she picked up the phone, removed the charging cord and opened the screen. Her mother had called several times, leaving voice and text messages, the latest one being just a few minutes ago. Landry immediately dialed her mother's number.

"I would say I'm glad I'm not dead, but that might sound too morbid," Astelle said the moment she picked up on her end.

Landry resisted the urge to frown and instead gave a cheery, "Hi, Mama."

"I've been calling you since last night," her mother continued. "Just because you're thousands of miles away, in the middle of some ocean, doesn't mean you cannot answer the phone. Or return a phone call in a timely fashion. I mean, really, Landry, there could have been an emergency."

And from that sentence alone Landry realized that there wasn't and she took a seat on the couch. "The battery in my phone died, so I didn't even see that you'd called until just now."

Her mother was technology challenged, so Landry knew that talking about her phone would get Astelle to take the conversation in another direction.

"Anyway, I wanted to tell you about the Singles' Social at the church," she said.

Landry laid her head back on the chair and dropped an arm over her forehead. Was her mother really calling her about church events when, as Astelle had so sweetly put it, she was thousands of miles away in the middle of some ocean?

Astelle continued, "Your father and I were talking yesterday morning and we thought it would be perfect if you could attend. Now, it's Saturday night and before you say it, I know that's tomorrow. But you should be able to get those fancy royal people to send you home on a plane so that you can attend. Paula said they probably have their own private jet. More than one actually. Anyway, don't worry about what to wear, I called Kelli and she can get you something from your studio."

It was official, her mother had finally completely lost her mind. Landry berated herself for thinking negatively about her mother. Especially since the scare she'd received concerning her parents before she'd left the States had almost been a deal breaker for her taking this job. Her father had been rushed to the hospital the day after Malayka offered Landry this position. The chest pains he'd been having were concerning enough to have him set up with cardiologists and other specialists within the week. Landry decided that night at the hospital that she would stay in LA. Her father had told her she would do no such thing.

Landry shook her head to clear that memory from her mind. Her mother had already said this wasn't an emergency call so there was no need to think back on that horrible time. Besides, Astelle had just gone quiet which meant she was now waiting for Landry's response.

"I cannot attend the event, Mama," Landry said after taking a deep breath and exhaling slowly. "I'm working here on Grand Serenity Island. The job isn't over until mid-December, after the royal wedding."

"Well, you don't work on weekends, do you?" her mother asked.

"Yes, I do."

Astelle huffed. "You shouldn't work yourself so hard, Landry. You're only given one life—you need to take the time to actually live it."

"I am living my life, Mama. I started this business because it was my dream. It's everything to me and I plan to work as hard as I can to make the best of it," she replied.

"There's more to life than work… Like socializing and giving yourself the chance to meet the right man," Astelle said.

Landry sighed inwardly wondering if her mother would ever talk about anything other than her finding a man and settling down.

"My job actually entails a lot of socializing," she rebutted.

"Oh really? Have you been going to fancy parties or exploring that lovely island with anyone in particular?"

She'd walked right into that one.

"The royal family has been very hospitable. The princess gave me a personal tour."

"That's nice. I hope you were respectful."

"I was, Mama."

"And who else? Didn't you say there was a prince?"

Landry rolled her eyes. Her mother couldn't remember how to install an app on her phone, but she wouldn't dare forget any mention of an eligible bachelor.

"There are two princes, Roland and Kristian. I've met both of them and they've been very pleasant as well," Landry informed her mother.

"Any sparks there? Between you and the princes?"

"Really, Mama. In one breath you want me to come home to attend a church social full of bachelors and in the next you ask if I'm flirting with not one, but both princes." Landry had to chuckle at that herself.

Astelle did not think it was funny. "That's not what I said. I simply asked if there were any sparks there, and I didn't mean with both of them. I was asking if there were sparks with either one."

"No," she replied, quickly.

Too quickly.

"Oh?" Astelle immediately perked up.

"Mama, I really have to get going. I'll call you Sunday night when you're back from church," Landry told her, praying she could get off the phone without giving away the fact that there were not only sparks between her and one of the princes, but that she'd actually just come from his bed.

"I see, well that's fine. You go on and get your work done. I suppose the sooner the job is finished the sooner you'll return home. If that's still the plan. So I'll just tell your father you won't be attending the social and we'll talk to you later. Bye now, and you take care of yourself down there," Astelle said.

"You and Daddy take care too," Landry said. "I love you both."

"We love you too, baby. Go on now, don't be late for what you have to get done. And be nice to everyone there, especially him."

Astelle hung up before Landry could ask her mother who "him" was. Landry was left to stare at her cell phone replaying their conversation in her mind.

If that's still the plan, Astelle had said. *Be nice...to him.*

Landry shook her head and fell back against the chair. Now her mother was thinking she had something going on with someone down here. That was just great. No, it wasn't. Her mother was wrong. Or was she?

She was wearing the clothes she'd had on yesterday, including the shirt with its elastic collar stretched out because Kris had decided to push the shirt down her body, instead of pulling it over her head. Her legs were still a little weak from the multiple times they'd made love throughout the night. Her hair was most likely a matted mess and her lips still tingled from the memory of his kisses.

Was there something going on between her and Kristian?

Now probably wasn't the greatest time to ask that question.

Chapter 10

"We'll have extended security for the Ambassador's Ball next weekend," Rafe said in response to Malayka's inquiry.

Kris had heard her question, every one of them since they'd sat down to dinner almost twenty minutes ago. In the last three weeks since the accident, Malayka had been very concerned about Rafe's safety. They all were. The difference was that Kris and his siblings were taking care of matters on their own. They weren't discussing this situation at the family dinner table and acting as if someone were going to break into the palace at any moment and shoot Rafe while he sat at the head of the table.

Glad that his father had answered her question, Kris finished his dessert and signaled to a staff member that he was ready for another glass of wine. Normally, he drank coffee after dinner, reserving the wine or anything stronger for when he was alone in his rooms. Tonight, he needed wine immediately.

It had been a long day, one where he'd tried to convince himself that these past weeks spent with Landry in his bed weren't such a bad idea. Since the first night that they were together Kris would either seek her out at the pool after dinner or send her a message that they were to meet in his rooms. They never spoke of any specifics to their newfound arrangement, nor did they look any further into the future than the next night that they could be in each other's arms.

This was a first for Kris, a clandestine affair, which seemed more like something Roland would do. He wasn't proud of it and yet, there was a big part of him that hated each morning when Landry would wake early and sneak out of his room. It made sense that she leave before the staff began moving around and could possibly witness her departure. Still, he hadn't been able to let go of the emptiness he'd felt each day when she was gone.

Luckily, or perhaps not, his daily schedule remained full, so it had been unusual for him to have the time to think about the situation with Landry throughout the day. Today, however, was different.

He had meetings throughout the day. The bank, the rescheduled meeting with Quirio about the massive resort he planned to build on the opposite side of the island and then the Skype conference call with the security guy Roland recommended. To tell the truth, if it weren't for Quirio's grand plans and the boost in tourism it would afford the island, Kris would say that all of his meetings had been a disaster.

Gerard Yiker was the former CIA agent who had connections all over the world. He seemed to be an astute man with no real allegiance to any country at this point in his life. He knew things and he knew how to barter them to people who required his intel. Kris did not want to bargain with the guy. He, his father and Rafe's father had sworn to never negotiate with terrorists. Now, Yiker might not be a terrorist in the simplest form of the word but the guy was definitely an extortionist. Which had Kris thinking he might just have someone else in mind who could help them.

After touring the site where Quirio wanted to build the resort, Tajeo had driven Kris directly to the bank for his meetings there. Those meetings had run longer than anticipated and instead of returning to the palace for his Skype call, Kris was forced to use his office there. It was just after the call wherein he'd informed Yiker that he would get back to him with a final answer about whether or not they would be using his services, that Kris noticed something wrong.

His office was located in the very back of the two-story building that housed the bank. The building was constructed with reinforced steel beams and triple-thick concrete. The windows were a bulletproof Plexiglas and there was an intricate alarm system on all the doors. That did not include the mechanisms designed to keep the main vault safe, or the secondary underground vault that no one but Kris, Rafe and the bank manager knew about. Every door inside the building required a key card to enter and thermal scanners were activated each time a person entered through the front and only entrance.

After being in his office for over an hour it was only when Kris had stood to leave that he noticed the plant on the floor near the window. Dirt had spilled out but the bright-colored flower was still rooted in the pot. Wondering why the cleaning staff hadn't taken care of this, he'd walked over to inspect the plant himself. As he knelt down he realized he could hear noise from the street. Between the windows and the extra-thick walls, outdoor sounds had never been able to be heard inside the building. Looking up, Kris realized why that wasn't true today. The window was open.

He stood slowly and reached into his back pocket for his cell phone.

"We've got a problem at the bank," he spoke into the phone as soon as he received an answer.

It hadn't taken long to get Salvin Gathersburgh, the chief guard from the palace, and Tajeo there to survey the scene. Kris had been thoroughly surprised to see Roland walk in as well.

"My text stated that everything was fine," Kris had said to his brother the minute he walked into the office.

Roland frowned. *"Your text stated you thought someone had broken into the bank, but that everything was fine. Who says that?"*

His brother was already walking toward the window, looking at the plant on the floor and then up to the open window.

"Was anything missing from in here?" Roland had asked Kris.

Kris shook his head. *"Nothing. I've checked twice. I have a safe over here beneath this portrait. It wasn't disturbed. Contents are still there."*

"We should check for any type of listening devices and get fingerprints," Salvin told them. *"Probably better if we call the police commander over to have a look too."*

"No," Roland and Kris had said simultaneously.

"Let's keep this under wraps for now. The citizens are still reeling from the accident. We don't need to cause any more panic by making them think that something illicit is going on," Kris stated, even though he was already feeling like they had a major problem.

So hours later, by the time he'd entered the dining room, Kris was in a less than festive mood. In fact, he'd really considered not attending the dinner at all, which would not go over well. Besides, the more he'd thought about skipping, the more he wanted to go, just to see Landry.

"I'm not sure it would look good to have too many guards standing out in the crowds. As you know I've contacted some of my press connections in the States. The first official event of the soon-to-be princess is a big deal for them," Malayka was saying.

Kris knew that if he looked over at her she'd have that gleaming smile she wore especially for the reporters.

"We should continue to use the same discretion with the press as we've done in the past," Sam stated. "I think it would be a good idea if we combine our list of media connections and have all of them vetted according to our usual standards."

"So you want me to run everything I do by you first? That doesn't sound correct. The chain of command…"

"The chain of command does not shift until you are married," Kris interrupted Malayka. "Until that time we have protocols in place and we will continue to use them."

When she dropped her fork to her plate and made a hissing sound, Rafe spoke up. "He's right. Now is not the time to change how we operate here. If you anticipate any extra press attending the event you need to provide their names and contact information to Sam. She knows what to do," he told her. "Actually, now would probably be a great time for her to show you everything she does."

Kris watched as his father extended his arm closing the distance between himself and Malayka by touching her hand. Malayka had been frowning—no, actually she'd been scowling at Sam—but as soon as Rafe touched her hand, her facial features softened and she sighed.

"I guess you're right," she replied.

"Maybe we should cancel the ball," Roland spoke up then.

"What? No! Now that is just too much. Tell him, Rafe," Malayka protested.

"In light of the accident and what happened—" Roland started before Kris interrupted.

"We are a united front. We do not flinch," Kris stated evenly.

He did not look at Roland as he spoke, or his father, but instead found himself staring directly at Landry.

She'd been toying with the whipped cream atop the white chocolate raspberry cheesecake they'd been served for dessert. Not eating it, just moving it around in a swirling motion that was turning it into a sopping white glob. She also appeared to be listening and Kris found it interesting that he wanted to know what she thought. Did she hate hearing these private family discussions? Was she as annoyed at Malayka's continuous talk about the princess-to-be as he was? Did she wonder why it all mattered?

Kris did. He wondered and he tried to keep it all in perspective. It was his job, after all.

"I'm not saying that this isn't serious," he continued, shifting his gaze to his brother. "We need to be on guard."

"What? Why?" Malayka asked and drew questioning looks from Sam, Roland and Kris. "Igor didn't check the brakes on the car. That wasn't a malicious attack. Why do we need to up the security and check out everyone we talk to like they're some type of government spy? And the Ambassador's Ball is a tradition. Right? We can't just stop traditions because of a car accident that didn't even kill anybody."

She was right, the car accident hadn't killed anyone. But it was meant to, and Kris wasn't totally certain what the break-in at the bank meant. To him, those were very good reasons to be on guard.

"The precautions are warranted, regardless of how harmless you believe the car accident was," Kris told her.

"Enough!" Rafe intervened. "I want to see the three of you in my office first thing tomorrow morning. Come, Malayka, we're retiring for the night."

Nobody spoke until they were gone, at which time Landry immediately pushed her chair back and stood.

"I should leave," she said.

"I'll walk you to your room," Roland offered.

Kris clenched his teeth and vowed to remain silent.

"No, thank you," she told him and then looked at Roland apologetically. "I mean, I can make it on my own. Besides, I believe there might be a discussion here once I'm gone that you should be part of."

Roland stood beside her then and lifted her hand to his mouth. "Very well, my dear. You win," he said before kissing the back of her hand.

She smiled as she slipped her hand from his, then turned to say good-night with a nod to him and to Sam. When she was gone his brother and sister looked directly to him.

"We're not canceling the ball and we're ramping up security. I'll say the same to Dad in the morning." Having said that Kris pushed his chair back and stood as well. He walked out of the dining room without another word.

It was a nice evening to think, Landry thought as she walked along the palace grounds. In the early days of being on the island she would spend her evenings with a relaxing swim, alone. Until that one night when everything changed. She'd known it the morning she crept out of his room that things were going to be different. But Landry hadn't realized how much so, not until now.

She'd slept with the crown prince. Not once, but over and over again, she'd spent hours in his bed, beneath him, on top of him, in the shower with him. Then, they would fall asleep in each other's arms, as if they were a real couple. Sighing, she pushed her hair back from her face and looked up to the evening sky. Damn stars and tropical-scented air, that's what had gotten her into trouble in the first place.

When she'd suggested that Kristian join her for some pizza it had only been to help him get through the scare of the accident. There'd been no thoughts to seduction or flirtation; she was certain of that fact. All she'd wanted was to make him feel better. Why, she still had no clue.

Why did it matter if Kristian DeSaunters looked happy or not? She shouldn't feel sorry for the somber way in which he lived his life. It was none of her business. Yet, she'd made it her business, at least for the past few weeks she had.

Landry hadn't lied to him, she had related to the fear he'd felt. When her father had fallen off a ladder and then again when he'd been rushed to the hospital with chest pains, she'd been terrified. So she knew what Kristian had been feeling that day. She knew and she'd tried to help.

Then why did she feel like she'd caused more harm? Because she probably had.

Malayka had met with her wedding coordinator today. They were interviewing caterers and entertainment for the reception. So Landry had time to herself. She stayed in her room in order to make calls and handle other business. She reviewed her finances and sent invoices to her accountant. After lunch she took a long nap and when she woke, caught up on some recent fashion articles.

She had not come out of her room all day.

That's why she was there when the delivery came.

"I wasn't expecting any shipments today," she told the staff members that carried the half dozen boxes into her room.

"It is for you," one of them had said before they both left her alone once more.

There was no name on the box and no cards attached to give a clue where or who they were from so she had no choice but to open one of them. Removing the lid and pushing aside the pastel-colored tissue paper Landry was momentarily speechless. It was a black-and-white blouse, an off-the-shoulder striped bell sleeve. After holding it up to survey it, Landry saw that there was another shirt in the box. This one, a very light tone of gray smocked-neck kimono cold-shoulder blouse. After pulling out all the tissue paper she was irritated to find there was still no card.

That meant she had to open another box, because surely if someone thought to send these to her, they'd at the very least want her to know who they were from.

There were two blouses in each box, a range of colors and styles, but all off-the-shoulder. Twelve of them. The room looked like there'd been a pastel explosion as she'd torn through each box looking for a card. She had found none.

As she stood there looking around and wondering what was going on, her cell phone chimed. It was a task finding the phone in the mess she'd created but eventually she did and saw that she had a text message.

I wanted to replace the top I ripped. I apologize. KRD

Landry read the message over again. He hadn't actually ripped her blouse that first night they were together, but the way he'd tried to take it off had stretched it out of shape. She'd never said a word about it, never asked him to buy her another blouse to replace that one.

She read the text a third time and her lips spread into a smile. She hadn't meant to, but there was a lightness in the pit of her stomach. A silly little rippling of pleasure at seeing his note and looking up at all those blouses.

Suddenly it became imperative to fold each blouse and lay them neatly in one of the drawers she was using. She broke the boxes down until they could be flattened and stacked on top of each other and found a bag in the bathroom that she could put all of the tissue paper into. In her travels throughout the palace she hadn't seen any recycle bins, but she was certain the royal family was concerned with protecting the environment. After showering and dressing for dinner she intended to find out where they kept their recycling and then thank Kristian the moment she saw him in the dining room.

She would thank him and then she would tell him that what they were doing was over.

That plan changed later, when she had entered the dining room and felt the tension. Everyone had watched her as she made her way to the table, offering an apology and a smile. Prince Rafe barely looked up at Landry and Malayka shook her head as if that sole action would admonish Landry for all her wrongdoing. The woman had really started to go on a power trip. Sam had smiled at her in return and Roland stood to pull her chair out for her. Kristian had looked at her and then hurriedly turned away.

That wasn't out of the ordinary. Since they'd been sleeping together, Kristian had made a concerted effort not to talk to her too much during dinners. A part of her had wanted to be angry about that fact, actually about the whole arrangement. Only she didn't remember agreeing to an affair with him. All she'd remembered was how her body had instantly heated at his touch, how his kisses wiped all coherent thoughts from her mind. It had been so good these past weeks and at the same time so very wrong.

Well, tonight, that was going to come to an end. After receiving those blouses from him this afternoon, Landry's mind had been made up. The very next time Kristian sent her one of his private messages, she was going to tell him it was over.

Now, after that tension-filled dinner, a lovely fragrance drew her down a stone pathway to where she could see large trees. A garden, she surmised and continued walking in that direction. Plants and flowers weren't really her thing, but the scents were enticing, almost soothing as she moved through the passageways. In daylight she presumed this garden would be gorgeous with the variety of flowers she saw and the neatly trimmed greenery. At this time of night everything was cast in a dull haze, but still, the effect of this seemingly endless path was breathtaking.

In the distance she could hear water, a slow trickle that added to this serene atmosphere. Landry walked toward the sound until she came to a clearing with expertly cut trees jutting high up into the sky and ponds lining the open area. Grass paths separated the ponds into neat squares, lily pads floating in each. It was gorgeous. Landry walked around one before kneeling and touching her fingers to the water.

"You love the water, don't you?"

She looked up to see Kristian standing on the other side of the pond, his hands tucked into his pant pockets, the action pushing his suit jacket back.

Flicking the water off her fingers as she came to stand, Landry shrugged. "It's relaxing."

"I guess," was his somber response.

He looked regal. No matter what he did or said that

royal air which surrounded him like a cloak could not be dismissed. It had Landry standing straighter, keeping eye contact and for once in her life making a valiant attempt to monitor her words. She had something to say to him and she'd rehearsed it in her mind for the past couple of hours. Still, when she spoke something totally different slipped out.

"What do you do to relax, Kristian?"

He stared for a few moments, as if he might not answer her at all. On several occasions when they'd been together she would do most of the talking. He would do most of the contemplating. She realized now that there were usually more questions than answers. That's what he did, she decided. He thought about each response, made sure what he said was exactly what he wanted to say. She'd have to learn that trick one of these days.

"I like to read," he replied finally.

He started to walk along one side of the pond and Landry followed by walking along the other side.

"What do you read?"

"Mythology. Folklore. History," he replied as casually as reciting the alphabet, instead of actually revealing something personal about himself.

"No romance or erotica?" she asked with a chuckle.

He remained quiet and she clasped her hands behind her back. She would definitely need much more practice in thinking about what she said before saying it.

"My mother used to read to me at night. Fairy tales that were filled with romance and sentiment. I learned very fast that the real world was nothing like a fairy tale and that romance and sentiment were not meant for a prince."

His words were cynical and sad. But Landry knew better than to voice those thoughts.

"I'm not a huge fan of fairy tales either," she stated. "But for different reasons than you, I suppose."

His reply came quicker this time. "Tell me your reasons."

They came to a grassy spot and Landry noted that all she had to do was take a few steps to her left and they would be standing side by side. Kristian continued to walk and so did she.

"Snow White was poisoned by an evil jealous queen and remained at death's door, until a prince came along and saved the day. As a result of yet another evil woman and her father's tyrannical ways, Sleeping Beauty also ended up in a death slumber, until, guess what? Another prince came around and saved her too." She shook her head and continued, "Cinderella inherited a castle and land but was forced to work like a slave because of an evil woman and her daughters. Until—"

"A prince came along and saved her as well," Kristian finished. "I see where you're going with this."

He chuckled lightly and Landry smiled.

"I'm just sayin' young girls can do without growing up believing that they need a man to 'save' them," she added. They could also do without almost falling for a man they had no business even thinking about.

"You would probably end up saving the man," he said, more seriously this time.

Landry shrugged again. "More shocking things have happened," she quipped.

"I'm not in a position to be saved."

"You create your own circumstances, control your own destiny. It doesn't have to be prewritten. Unless you want it to be."

Again, she probably should not have said that to him, and yet, a part of her wondered if Kristian was reaching out for someone to save him. What if he did feel trapped by his title, by this gorgeous island and all that came with it? There could be less appealing trappings, she thought.

They came to the end of the path where those same tall trees that lined the sides of the walkway crossed over and formed a wall. In front of that wall were two stone benches. Kristian took long strides until he turned and sat on one. Extending an arm he said quietly, "Come here."

Landry walked to him without thinking of whether or not she should. His legs were parted and when she took his hand, he pulled her down to sit on his lap.

"I thought about you today," he said, his gaze focused ahead, his arm going around her waist.

She swallowed hard, trying to adjust to the quick jolt of heat that soared through her body at their proximity.

"I thought of you while I was in meetings. When I rode along the winding roads in the car. As I dressed for dinner. When you came into the dining room, I tried not to stare at you. The entire time Malayka talked and when the sweetness of the dessert tickled the back of my throat. I cannot seem to stop thinking about you."

His voice was still quiet, the sound of the ocean in the distance, almost louder than his words. Yet, Landry had heard each one and she'd tensed as if she were naked in front of a ballroom full of people. His words were raw and…what really shocked her, honest.

"I thought of you when I sat in my room today. I tried to work but I couldn't forget where I was, whose house this is or the way back to your room. None of those things are what I should be thinking while I'm here."

They were quiet, because Landry did not know what he was going to say next. All she knew was that as his arm tightened around her waist, she leaned in closer to the wall of his chest. It was warm there, comfortable, easy.

"I said before that you weren't supposed to be here. Nowhere in the plan for my life did an American woman appear. Then I opened that folder and your picture stared back at me. You've been here," he said, lifting his free hand to tap a finger against his temple, "ever since that day. Stuck in my mind and then for the past weeks, in my arms. I don't know why, but I like that. I like it a lot."

That hand came down from his face to cup her jaw, turning her so that she was now staring directly into his eyes. "I like it a lot," he repeated.

"I like it too," she whispered as he pulled her in even closer. In her mind she heard her words replay and a part of her wanted to scream. She did not like being his dirty little secret. Her body, on the other hand, loved it.

Their lips touched lightly, slowly, once and then again. The third time his were parted. She knew they would be and she was ready. Their tongues touched lightly, sweetly. They touched again and twirled around in an enticing motion. His hand slipped around her neck to cup the back of her head, tilting it so that she would fall deeper into the kiss. Her hands moved up the lapels of his jacket, feeling the rise and fall of his muscled chest beneath, until she wrapped her arms around his neck. With an arm still around her waist, he pulled her even closer against him, their breathing growing quicker, louder.

Kris kissed her as if his next breath depended on their contact. His fingers tingled as they moved over the curve of her buttocks and the warm skin at the nape of her neck. She smelled like flowers, or was it the air surrounding them? He couldn't tell, all he knew was that he enjoyed it very much.

He'd liked how she had looked when she walked into the dining room. The simple, yet alluring, style of the dress that looked like a white dress shirt, belted at the waist, showing off her knees and legs. Her hair was pulled back from her face, held together by some sort of band. She'd taken his breath away without even trying.

Finding her here in his mother's garden had been a shock and for a moment he'd felt like it was an intrusion. Tonight he'd wanted to be alone, to gather his thoughts on what was going on in his mind. Then he'd watched her touch that water and he'd wanted her hands on him. He needed her on him, right now.

With a groan of resistance, Kris tore his mouth away. He kept his gaze on hers, watching the way the growing passion had filled her eyes and his fervent kisses left her lips plump and delectable. Reaching into his back pocket he pulled out his wallet and retrieved a condom. Her gaze didn't waver but he knew she was certain of what he was doing. Setting his wallet on the bench beside them, he handed her the condom and then planted his hands around her waist and lifted her up into his lap. She moved in conjunction with his every thought. Turning to face him as she ripped the condom package open, setting the paper on the bench beside his wallet as she straddled his lap.

Kris undid his pants and released his erection. She eased the condom down on his length. He cupped her face in his palms, pulling her down so that he could have her lips again. This kiss was hungry, a taking that said all the words neither of them decided to speak. She was moving, pushing at her dress. He continued to kiss her, but let his hands fall down to her legs. He loved the feel of her skin and dragged his hands slowly up her legs, hating to stop the contact. When he felt the hem of her panties he moved farther until his palms were now cupping her bottom. He squeezed both cheeks loving the sexy purring sounds she made in response. When she circled her hips it was Kris's turn to make noise. He groaned with pleasure and before he could stop himself, he grabbed the material of her panties and ripped them off.

His fingers trembled as they moved between her legs to feel the already wet and plump folds.

"Kristian," she whispered when he touched her there.

He sucked her tongue deeper into his mouth as he pressed his fingers slowly inside her. At the feel of her honeyed walls contracting around his fingers, Kris's body went into overdrive. He pulled those fingers quickly from her and held on to her hips, lifting her until she could come down quickly over his length.

It was sexy as hell, the way she slithered down onto him, her tongue still moving erotically in his mouth. Kris held her tighter, gritting his teeth at the pleasure of being fully ensconced in her heat. His thrusts came quickly after that. She tore her mouth away from his, breathing heavily as she arched her back and circled her hips to match his rhythm.

Pleasure came in sharp pricks against his skin, as if a million darts were being thrown at him all at once. He couldn't think, couldn't speak, he could only feel. She'd wrapped her legs completely around his waist, locking her ankles at his back. He sat up straighter to hold her and to keep them both leveraged as he pounded into her. When her fingers dug into his shoulder and his name became a litany of murmurs and sighs on her lips, Kris thought he would lose it immediately.

She was tight around him, her thighs trembling as she made the climb to her release. He leaned in, licking over the part of the material that covered her breasts. Then he nipped there, wanting desperately to feel her turgid nipple in his mouth once more. He didn't want to take his hands off her, loved the feeling of her bare cheeks in his palms as he moved quickly in and out of her. So he continued to suckle her breasts through the dress, until she made a sound that matched the jerking and stilling of her hips.

With her release came a surge of heat in Kris's body that he knew he'd never be able to explain. He felt as if that heat boiled instantly until there was a blast and before he knew what to say or how to react, he was groaning with his release. By now he was squeezing her so tightly, he was certain it must be painful.

He lowered his forehead until it rested on her chest. She was panting. He was panting. He loosened his grip only slightly on her. She flattened her palms on the back of his head, rubbing slowly as he leaned on her trying to catch his breath.

"Thank you."

He heard the words but wasn't totally sure she should be saying them.

"For what?" he asked without daring to look up at her.

If she was thanking him for sex, Kris wasn't going to be happy. As his mind began to clear of the foggy remnants of release, he wasn't actually feeling jubilant at the moment.

"For the blouses," she said. "I meant to thank you at dinner, but you left. And then you were here and before I could say it…well, just thank you."

Kris closed his eyes to her words, but still did not look up at her. She was thanking him for sending her a dozen shirts when he was pretty sure he was on his way to ruining her life.

How was he supposed to respond to that?

Chapter 11

"You're leaving me again," he said.

Landry had just finished smoothing down loose strands of her hair. Moments ago she'd slipped off his lap and adjusted her dress. As for the remnants of her underwear, she'd stuffed them into the front pocket of her dress and was prepared to make the uncomfortable trek to her bedroom commando-style.

She hadn't been facing him but when he spoke, she turned slowly.

"It's become a habit," she replied. "Leaving without being seen so I don't cause any trouble." The words were bitter in her mouth.

He'd adjusted his clothes as well, and he'd picked up his wallet and the condom paper from the bench. She presumed he'd also disposed of the used condom, but didn't want to think about where or how. Actually, Landry decided, she really just wanted to go back to her room.

"You believe that being with me might cause trouble?"

She almost laughed at the way he managed to sound oblivious to what was going on. "Maybe not trouble, but certainly confusion. At least for me."

"Then why do you do it?"

It took a moment for her to see that he was serious. "You mean, why do *we* do it? I don't know," she told him. "Gluttons for punishment, I suppose."

"Hmm, punishment," Kristian continued. "I hadn't actually thought of it that way."

She took a tentative step toward him and then stopped. Her thoughts were much clearer when she wasn't so close to him. Now was as good a time as any to get this conversation over with. So what they'd just had pretty terrific sex; it was always like that with them.

"How are you thinking of this, Kristian? What do you think we're doing?"

She really wanted him to answer this time because she was so not sure what was going on between them. It had happened so quickly, the change from him and her, to them, together, that she hadn't been able to make any sense of it.

"We're adults," he told her.

"You're right, we are."

"And…dammit!" he yelled, turning away from her.

Stunned for a few seconds at the outburst, Landry could only stare at him, until finally she decided to close the space between them.

"I didn't plan this. I only came here to do a job," she said standing behind him. "And I don't really know how or why it started."

"But it can't continue," he said, whirling around to face her again.

They were standing close this time, so close she could see the twitch of a muscle in his jaw.

"Is that what you're about to say? Or no, perhaps it was more along the lines of we should just go with this. Press on and see where it takes us," he was saying.

Landry didn't like his tone or his words. She squared her shoulders and cleared her throat. "No. What I'm saying is that I don't believe in games. We're attracted to each other, okay, we cannot deny that. I'm usually good at handling any type of relationship and rolling with the punches. But I've never been good at games. As for what would happen beyond the nights we keep spending together, I hadn't thought about it much, not until now."

"I have," he replied tersely. "I've thought about you and us and the inevitability of it all. We're too different, yet the attraction is undeniable."

Landry took a step back at that point, nodding her head as she considered her words.

"You're right again, Kristian. You're a prince and I'm just an American entrepreneur. Those differences are huge and yes, they too are undeniable."

He opened his mouth to say something and then shook his head. "That's not how I meant it," he told her.

"It is and that's fine because like I said, it's true."

He tried again. "We have different lives. We're meant to do different things."

"In other words, I'm a commoner and you're royalty."

"I didn't say that," he quickly replied.

Landry waited a beat and then gave a wry smile. "You didn't deny it either."

He sighed heavily. "Look, you just don't understand the situation I'm in. You have no idea the duties resting on my shoulders, the responsibility that I have to this country and to my family. I can't let her down—I just can't."

"You can't let who down?"

That muscle ticked in his jaw again and silence filled the air.

"Nothing," he finally replied. "You're right. It won't look good for either of us to be seen together like this. You leave first and go back to your room. I'll walk out in a few minutes."

"So that's that—we'll have these little hookups and then we scuttle off in our different directions in secret."

When he looked like he would respond, Landry raised a hand to stop him.

"No need for any more explanations. You've tried that already. We're too different and that's fine. I'm not some starry-eyed girl with dreams of marrying a prince and living in a palace. I've never wanted a serious relationship and least of all one where I would have to compromise my lifestyle for that of a title. I'll just head back to my room now, Your Highness. But please, do me a favor, no more text messages, no more gifts and no more nights like this."

Kristian didn't say another word, nor did he try to stop her. The latter, Landry discovered as she walked back to her room, had hurt the most.

"Good evening," Malayka spoke from behind Landry.

Landry turned so fast after entering her bedroom, and bit back a scream. With her back flattened against the door to her rooms, she stared at Malayka who was sitting with her legs crossed in an oatmeal-color tufted armchair.

"Ah, good evening. Did we have a meeting this late?" Landry asked when she finally got herself together enough to move away from the door and walk farther into the room.

"I'll ask the questions, if you don't mind. Where were you last night? I called you and I came to your room.

You're supposed to be at my beck and call, and you weren't here."

Landry moved slowly, still uncomfortable from her lack of underwear and not in the mood for conversation with her client. She took a seat in the chair that was positioned directly across from Malayka.

"I don't think our contract says anything about *beck and call*," Landry stated in a voice as calm as she could muster after walking quickly down a long hallway only to be frightened by an uninvited guest in her room. "And before you go on, yes, I know that you are about to become the princess of this beautiful island. My job is to dress you for all of your functions leading up to that time. We both have a calendar with those important dates listed. I schedule meetings and fittings with you and I'm present for every one of them. I am doing my job."

Malayka opened her mouth to reply, but Landry shook her head and held up a finger to stop her.

"Just one more thing," she told the soon-to-be princess. "I do not appreciate you letting yourself into my room and questioning me like I'm a child. Now, is there something else?"

Again, Astelle Norris's voice echoed in Landry's head. She'd said too much, and she hadn't monitored her tone. She'd been *sassy*, which was one of Astelle's favorite words to describe Landry. Landry didn't care. Malayka was the type of person who needed to be nipped in the bud sooner, rather than later. If Landry answered the woman's questions tonight without telling her that she was stepping over their professional line, then Malayka would feel as if she could treat Landry any way she wanted to. True, Malayka or rather—as evidenced from her latest check—Prince Rafferty was paying Landry's invoices, so she owed them a measure of respect. But no amount of zeroes on a check would ever mean that Landry was going to tolerate disrespect from anyone.

Malayka didn't move a muscle. Her hair was pulled back from her face with a jeweled band, the sage-colored dress she'd worn at dinner falling to her ankles, gold strappy sandals at her feet. It was a lovely outfit, which Malayka had managed to select for herself.

"This is my house," Malayka began, keeping her saccharine-filled smile in place. "I have a right to know all the comings and goings around here. Besides, I'm concerned for you."

Landry wanted to laugh. From the way that Malayka was looking at her to the blatant lie she'd just told, the scenario was more than a little funny. Instead, she decided she could play this game too, for just a moment.

"Really? Why are you concerned about me?" she asked.

"I've noticed how you've been looking at Kristian."

A jolt of surprise speared through her. Still, Landry kept her face and her response as indecipherable as possible.

"How exactly have I been looking at him?" Landry asked.

Malayka uncrossed her legs then and leaned forward keeping her gaze locked on Landry's.

"You want him," Malayka said candidly. "And before you deny it, let me tell you that it's no secret around the palace that you've been attending every dinner in the main dining room, whereas no other staff has ever been invited. Samantha did her normal tour of the island with you. Roland paid a bit of attention to you. So you may be thinking that you have a chance. But let me tell you right here and now, you don't."

It was hard to digest Malayka's words as her body still tingled in every spot that Kristian had just touched. He'd been rougher tonight than last night and the nights before that, but Landry had loved it just the same. Yet, this woman was telling her she couldn't have a man that Landry had already had, on more than one occasion to be exact.

"He's taken," Malayka continued before Landry could figure out what to say and how best to say it. "Her name is Valora Harrington and she's been betrothed to Kristian since they were both children. They're both natives to this island. The citizens know and love them and expect them to be married, as their fathers agreed upon long ago. So, you see, there's no room for an American entrepreneur in this picture."

Landry did not know what to say. She did not know how to feel. What she did know, however, was that there was no way she was giving Malayka the satisfaction of seeing her stumble.

"I hope Prince Rafferty is doing well this evening. I'm sure these past few weeks have been stressful to him." While Malayka looked surprised that Landry had completely changed the subject, Landry continued. "I'm expecting the last few dresses for you to arrive tomorrow. I've already planned a fitting for tomorrow afternoon. If you'd rather reschedule for another time in the next couple of days, I completely understand. You probably want to spend as much time with your fiancé as possible."

"Fine," Malayka said as she stood.

Landry stood as well, keeping the small smile she'd managed to muster.

"We'll keep our appointment," she told Landry. "And you just remember to keep your distance."

"Los Angeles is a good distance away, Malayka. As soon as our contract is up that's where I'll be. So you can save your warnings for the next woman who crosses your path," Landry told her.

"Right," Malayka said with a nod. "Am I trying on the

Peta Romanti dress tomorrow? She did say she was sending an original for the wedding festivities, right?"

Landry gave a quick nod as she followed Malayka to the door. "Yes, she did. It should be in tomorrow's shipment."

"I was under the impression that you had a personal connection to her," Malayka said when she opened the door.

Or else she might not have been hired? That's what Landry figured Malayka was attempting to say. Again, she wanted to laugh. The only reason Peta had agreed to send a dress for Malayka was because of Landry and also because Malayka was engaged to a prince. Otherwise, that picture that Peta had taken with Malayka over a year ago would have been the extent of the designer's contact with the soon-to-be princess.

"I've known Peta for a few years now and she never lets me down," Landry replied. "It's important to keep good professional relationships in this business."

"Exactly," Malayka said as she turned to give Landry one more sweet smile. "See you tomorrow, Landry."

"See you tomorrow, Malayka."

Their exchange had been weird and mostly uncalled for, except that it had added one more strike to the column of Landry's mistakes.

Chapter 12

The room was empty.

Malayka was late for their appointment. Landry found that to be almost laughable especially considering the condescending tone Malayka had last night in her room.

"He knows to follow my instructions. He'll do what he's paid to do or I'll find someone else to do it," was what Landry heard the moment she'd pushed the rack of dresses into Malayka's new dressing room. Landry didn't understand why a second dressing room had been necessary, but she'd known better than to open that door of discussion. All she wanted to focus on today was her job.

Her deliveries had arrived on schedule. After checking each package, she'd placed each dress on the rack and made her way to the far end of the hall past Malayka's rooms.

The voice belonged to a male and wasn't one that Landry was familiar with. That meant nothing consider-

ing there were at least fifty staff members moving throughout the palace at one time or another. Falling back on her
no eavesdropping rule, Landry continued to move around
the space getting things together for Malayka's impend-
ing arrival.

The gown from Detali was zipped in a black garment
bag. Landry went into the closet where all the new shoes
that had been shipped over from the United States were
being stored. She walked up and down the narrow path
between the shelves looking for just the right shoes to go
with the dress.

"You're not the boss! I get my orders directly from him
and then they filter down to you. Don't make me sorry I
picked you."

It was that guy's voice again.

She figured he was in the room right next to this one
but for whatever reason Landry could hear him entirely
too clearly. When she came out of the shoe closet and felt
a cool breeze she realized why. The doors to the balcony
in this room had been left open. Gauzy white curtains
were lifted off the floor as another breeze sifted through.
Malayka didn't like feeling too stuffy and she swore this
room did not receive the same force of air-conditioning
that her bedroom did.

The fact that this was a five-hundred-year-old palace
probably had something to do with that. While Landry had
seen the rectangular-shaped air-conditioning units positioned along the top line of the walls in most of the rooms
in the palace, she knew there were some rooms that did
not have any air at all. It hadn't surprised or annoyed her,
maybe because she had read all about the history of this
palace and the island in the time that she'd been there. She
was certain Malayka hadn't done that.

As excited as Landry had been this time yesterday

morning about today's fitting, at the moment, she simply wanted to get it over with. The little bombshell—that was actually more like a gigantic monkey wrench—Malayka had dropped on her last night was still rolling around in her mind.

Kristian was engaged to be married.

With a sigh, and because she could still hear that voice that was doing nothing to drown out her thoughts, Landry approached the balcony doors. More of the neighboring conversation played, just in case she did want to listen attentively.

She did not, still she stepped out on the balcony and saw a man with his back turned to her on the connecting balcony. He wore a white shirt and white slacks and a white baseball cap. Landry still wasn't sure who he was or who he was talking to as he looked toward the doors and said, "I'll be done with this call in a second."

"Nine o'clock," he continued saying. "Not a moment before or after. I don't have to tell you what will happen if you mess this up."

Figuring she definitely did not want to know what was going on at nine o'clock, Landry moved back inside and closed the balcony doors. Snapping the lock into place, she walked away telling herself that she shouldn't have been listening to something that wasn't her business. After all, she had no idea who was talking anyway.

Her business was getting this dress approved so that in several more days Malayka could walk into the ballroom wearing a Detali original and stun everyone in the room. Landry knew for a fact there would be press at the Ambassador's Ball. In addition to the local reporters, Malayka had been sure to issue a press release to the international media. She'd invited Hollywood producers and Wall Street giants, US and European politicians and their wives. It was as if this were the actual wedding, Landry thought when she'd watched Malayka working her own press coverage. But the soon-to-be princess was adamant about documenting her rise to the throne on a national level.

So, for Landry, that meant Detali Designs would also go national, and with it, Landry's name. A win-win for all involved, she told herself as she checked her watch. Malayka was now very late.

Landry was annoyed.

She could be doing other things besides waiting in this room for Malayka to show up whenever she felt like it. She could be in her room kicking herself for being an idiot.

How could she have slept with someone who was engaged to be married? Well, that answer was pretty simple. She didn't know Kristian was engaged. Nothing she'd read in the papers had mentioned it and nobody had thought to tell her that important fact. Or rather, it had never occurred to Landry to ask the question. So naive of her to presume that if he were coming on to her that he must be single. She'd thought he was available, just like her. Oh how wrong she'd been.

No wonder he seemed to be struggling with what they were doing; he was cheating. She sighed, so tired of thinking about this over and over again. "I hope those dresses arrived. I'm not going to be a happy camper if they haven't," Malayka said as she breezed into the room.

Cheryl McCoy, her makeup artist and Amari Taylor, the hair stylist, followed. Landry had seen these two before, which meant she'd witnessed their superior brand of ass kissing, on more than one occasion. Yet another thing she was not in the mood for today.

"The dresses are here. We can get started right away," Landry said as she moved to the rack.

"I hope you pick something colorful," Cheryl spoke with too much excitement. "I'd love to do something lavish with your eyes for this event."

"I don't think *lavish* is a word that should be attached to a princess," Landry mumbled.

Or at least she thought she'd mumbled. As it turned out the others had heard her and after she unzipped the first garment bag she looked over her shoulder to see them staring at her critically. With a shrug she continued to take the first dress out of the bag.

"It's black." Cheryl sighed.

"Black is timeless," Amari added.

He came closer to the rack and reached out to touch the fabric.

"Ooohwee, and it's satin. That's going to lie nicely over your body, Layka." Amari looked over Landry's shoulder with a grin on his face.

He was a tall man, slim and willowy. His thick eyebrows were perfectly arched and definitely the envy of women all over the world. His wavy hair was cut short, hairline shaped precisely. He wore two diamond stud earrings and black nail polish on two fingers on each hand.

"Satin is so ordinary," Malayka replied.

Landry was removing the gown when she turned to see that Malayka—thankfully—had stepped behind the screens to the left of the room.

"Let's decide when we see you in this masterpiece," Amari continued.

He attempted to take the dress off the hanger, with every intention of walking it over to Malayka, and quite possibly going behind the screen to help her put it on. But Landry gave him a look. Yes, one cool and no-nonsense look that had the man pursing his lips and taking a step back while folding his arms over his chest. She didn't give his theatrics the glory of a reply, instead she carried the dress over to the screen and handed it to Malayka.

"This is the Dolce & Gabbana. We sent the first two back, so this is the special order," Landry told Malayka.

Ten minutes later, Malayka had come out to stand in front of the mirror, turning this way and that and getting more opinions than Landry thought were necessary. Her client sighed and told her once more, "Send it back."

Three dresses and an hour and a half later, Landry was rewarded with, "This dress is brilliant!"

If Landry were in a better mood she might have jumped for joy at that exclamation. Malayka turned, looking over her shoulder to see her backside reflection in the free-standing mirrors.

"Yes! That dress is fiyah!" Amari declared and began clapping his hands.

Cheryl was nodding as she smiled. "I'm gonna have a great time with your makeup. Cannot wait until that ball. You're going to be the best-looking soon-to-be princess the people of this island have ever seen!"

Landry didn't speak. She couldn't because the dress was perfect. It was gorgeous and glamorous, unique and just like Amari had said...fiyah!

And it was the Detali original.

Malayka Sampson had just made her day.

Skipping dinner was probably cowardly.

And foolish, Landry thought as she took another bite of the granola bar she'd found in the bottom of her purse.

Six more months and she would be leaving this island and all its picturesque beauty. Including the lovely scene ahead of her at the moment. The Cliffs. Landry had read about them in one of the pamphlets she'd picked up when she'd traveled to the City Center in search of a place to

mail postcards to her mother. Astelle collected postcards
from wherever she went in the world, from tiny towns to
big cities. The only postcard her mother had from an actual island was the one Landry had bought her from Saint
Bart's when she'd flown there to assist one of her clients
on a photo shoot. Landry was excited to share the pretty
cards she'd purchased in one of the quaint little gift shops
near Grand Serenity's port.

She'd found the courier's office and mailed over a dozen
cards home to her mother, imagining the smile on her face
when she received them. Then Landry had returned to the
palace. Restless, she wasn't ready for bed and couldn't bear
being stuck in her rooms another minute. So she'd called
the number that Jorge had given her and asked him to meet
her at the front entrance.

After weeks of being in the palace she'd noticed that everyone left from the back of the property where the garage
was. She'd asked Jorge to pick her up in the front once and
prayed that he wouldn't run back and tell Kristian or the
others about her strange request. Instead he'd simply done
as she'd asked. That had earned him an ice cream cone
that Landry had bought from a beautiful shop in town.

If Jorge wondered why she'd called him again so quickly
tonight, he hadn't mentioned it. He simply picked her up
and asked where she wanted to go. When she'd said The
Cliffs he'd nodded and told her she would love the view
from there.

He hadn't lied. The view was magnificent. Landry had
no idea how high up she was but she was standing on the
peak of a cliff. Smooth rock was visible beneath her feet;
not too far behind patches of grass and shrubbery grew.
Down below, far down below, the water was still bright
turquoise and clear. At least it would have been if it were
daylight. As darkness had already fallen over the island,

the water still had a crystalline quality as it shimmered against the edge of the rocks. In the distance she could see boats, their lights like a beacon in the otherwise darkness.

Wrapping her arms around her chest, Landry stood perfectly still, looking out to sea as she inhaled the sweet island air. She liked it here, she finally admitted. The slow lifestyle and the friendly people. She loved walking down the cobblestone streets in the City Center and looking at the quaint and colorful buildings that crowded the square. When she stood there she only had to tilt her head up slightly to see more colorful dwellings tucked into the mountainside as if nature had put them there. It was majestic and amazing, soothing and invigorating all at the same time.

"Just when you thought you'd made a grand escape."

Landry jumped and turned, taking a hurried step away from the edge of the cliff before she actually tumbled over, and stared into Roland's laughing eyes.

In contrast to his brother, Roland always seemed to be happy. Except last night he'd seemed irritated at dinner and then again at the press conference she'd watched on television that afternoon, then he'd appeared contemplative and serious. The press conference was a follow-up to the accident. The police chief had spoken, but Kristian had stood right beside him, his face a mask of consternation. It was, of course, a handsome face, but Landry had been more drawn to the sadness that always seemed to cloud his eyes.

Roland had stood beside Kristian, both men dominant in their own way.

"Not trying to escape," she told him with a slight smile. "Just needed some air."

"Hey, I get it," he said, moving closer to where she stood. "With over fifteen bedrooms, two gourmet kitchens and three, not one or two, but three, ballrooms, the palace definitely has a shortage of air."

He chuckled and Landry balled the granola bar paper in her hand.

"We also have food in those two gourmet kitchens. Unless you're on some type of granola diet."

Landry laughed this time.

"You're not like the others. I forget that until I'm in your presence," she admitted.

He shrugged.

"Well, you know, I do my best."

He smelled good. A musk fragrance that was stronger than Kristian's cologne. It fit Roland's bold and brash personality. So did the black dress jeans, fitted beige shirt and black denim jacket he wore.

"You do, don't you," she said. "I mean, you try really hard to be the complete opposite of what others believe you are."

"People shouldn't judge based on what they see and hear. I'm under no obligation to appease them in that fashion," he said.

She nodded because she'd taken that same stance in her own life. Landry refused to act the way her parents wanted her to in order to get and keep a man. She had goals and aspirations and had worked her way to checking each of those little boxes off her to-do list without caring who thought it was a good idea or not.

"I agree," she said. "But then again, I'm not a prince. I'm certain the rules are different for you."

"Why? Because I happened to be born into a family of rulers? If you hadn't noticed, we don't get to select our parents," he said.

"That's for sure," she replied.

"What? You don't like your parents?"

"To the contrary, I love them. I'm not sure they love me all the time, but that's a discussion for another day," she quipped, "or night, I guess."

"Well," he said as he came close enough to wrap and arm around her shoulder and pull her close to him. "We should definitely spend some more time together as it appears we may have something in common."

"What? You have a dysfunctional relationship with your family too? I would have never guessed that one."

Roland had begun walking them down the hill. Landry had been ready to leave, but she liked talking to him.

"With my father, my sister and, oh yeah, my brother," he told her.

"Why? Because he's a liar?" Landry stopped immediately, clapping a hand over her mouth. Dammit, she'd done it again!

"Whoa, what did you just say?"

Landry shook her head, unable to trust herself this time.

"Kris lied to you? About what?"

"It's nothing," she said and continued walking. "Besides, I wouldn't call it a lie since I never asked the question. I guess it's more of an omission."

"And what did my perfect big brother omit?"

"It doesn't matter," she insisted.

"Obviously it does," Roland countered.

He touched her elbow, holding her until she stopped moving. Landry sighed.

"I didn't know he was betrothed," she said with exaggeration to that last word. She hated that word.

"Betrothed? Kris?" Roland shook his head, then stopped. "Oh, you're talking about Valora and that crazy deal her father keeps insisting was made."

"He should have told me that he was promised to someone else. Marrying someone else. Or I should have guessed

because isn't that what royals do?" There was a tree behind her and Landry decided to use it because she was ex-
hausted from thinking about Kristian all day. She leaned
back and scrubbed her hands over her face.

"First, he's not obligated to mention something that
doesn't exist. Valora's father is an old drunk who loves to
gamble. When he was younger—and still drinking quite
heavily—he played a game of poker with my aging and
already sick grandfather. My father said that Valora's dad
cheated. Of course, Valora's dad says he did not and that
my grandfather lost. The payout was a royal union—a
DeSaunters son promised to his daughter, whenever they
were born."

She stared at him incredulously then. "What? Are you
serious?"

Roland nodded. "It's never been true, but Valora's father
tells anyone who'll listen that it is. That's why so many is-
landers believe it to be true, I suppose."

"Why hasn't anyone in your family set the record
straight?"

"The people of Grand Serenity are a romantic sort,"
Roland told her.

He was standing in front of her now, one hand in his
front pant pocket, while he rubbed the other hand down
the back of his head.

"They look at the palace and the people who live here
and believe all the fairy tales they've ever read. Marriages
are arranged—good matches are made via good families.
Valora's grandfather fought for my grandfather's army so
while they aren't of royal status, there is loyalty there."

"Loyalty," Landry said. "But not enough to really have
her and your brother getting married."

"Kris would never agree to an arranged marriage. He's
too stubborn for something like that. And Valora, she's as

headstrong as my sister. No way those two were ever going to be told who to marry and when."

Landry didn't know what to believe. All she knew at this moment was that she had one heck of a headache and she was still hungry.

"I'm sorry. I shouldn't have called him names and I definitely should not have been talking about him to you," she said and pushed away from that tree. "I'll be heading back to the palace now."

"What's your hurry?" Roland said. "I was just heading out for a little fun, ah… I mean, air. I needed to get some air too."

He was grinning and Landry liked his grin. Kristian wasn't engaged to be married, but she still had no business thinking about him or sleeping with him for that matter. What better way to get those thoughts out of her head than to hang out with Roland for a couple of hours.

"Well, I'm sure if anyone knows where the best 'air' is on this island, it would be you."

"You're absolutely right about that," Roland told her. "I know just the spot for us to get that air and to talk more about why you were so irritated by the notion that Kris would be engaged and not tell you."

Landry opened her mouth to rebut that statement but something told her the action would be futile.

Chapter 13

It was Friday night, and Landry felt like a princess.

Never in all her years of loving fashion and dressing people had she ever imagined feeling the way she did tonight.

After the week she'd had, going to the Ambassador's Ball had been far from her mind. Ordinarily, it wasn't always her practice to attend the events she dressed her clients for. However, as she'd discovered in the past week, this wasn't an ordinary assignment.

The last five days had been full of ordering shoes and accessories and praying they would be delivered on time. There had been two more fittings to make sure the Detali dress was a perfect fit for Malayka. She'd skipped a few more dinners in the dining room and avoided Roland's knowing glances and comments. She hadn't, however, been able to avoid Prince Rafe when he'd decided that he wanted to speak to her.

On Tuesday, he'd surprised her by sitting at one of the huge quartz-topped islands in the kitchen when she'd been returning from another recycle run.

"You are very conscientious," he'd said the moment she appeared through the doorway.

Dressed in old jeans and a faded T-shirt, Landry had been shocked and a little embarrassed to be in the prince's company looking disheveled and tired. She didn't have a mirror directly in front of her but the way she'd been feeling that day certainly showed.

"Just trying to do my part," she replied with a small smile. *"Having a snack?"* Holding a conversation hadn't really been her idea, but simply walking away from him wasn't an option either.

"Doctor says I should watch my sugar intake. Eat more fruits and vegetables, he says," Rafe spoke as he looked down at the bowl of fruit in front of him. *"Last time I checked all this fruit had a ton of natural sugar."*

Landry had stepped a little closer to the island and peeped into the bowl. Strawberries, blackberries, kiwi, red grapes and mandarin oranges. The salad looked tasty and refreshing to her, but the prince did not seem impressed.

"I believe that natural sugar is better for you than refined sugars. At least that's what they told my dad the last time he was in the hospital," she said.

"Your father is sick?" Rafe asked. He put his fork down beside the bowl and looked up to her, clearly dismissing that fruit salad.

Landry quickly shook her head because she hated even voicing those words. *"He's doing well now,"* she replied. *"Two months ago, however, he had a health scare. The doctors suggested he change his diet and cutting out refined sugars was one thing on the list. He was grumpy about it, just like you."*

A chuckle had bubbled up from her chest inadvertently and when she would have clapped her mouth shut and tried to make a speedy getaway, Rafe stopped her by laughing with her.

"I guess you could say I'm grumpy about eating a bowl full of fruit," he admitted. *"We don't grow a lot of fruit here on the island because of the climate. It has to be imported, which, along with exporting, is a steadily developing part of our economy."*

Landry nodded, recognizing the way his duties comingled with his personal life, just like Kristian's.

"It's important to eat healthy, especially when your health is at risk. Your constituents would be very encouraged by seeing you eat this salad and take control of your health and well-being."

"Are you suggesting I start a healthy eating campaign?"

"Oh no," she said, shaking her head now. *"I was just making an observation. But I know it's none of my business. I tend to talk too much sometimes."*

Most times, she told herself. She'd especially talked too much to Roland who now knew that something had happened between her and Kristian. No, she had not shared any specifics but it had been pointless to deny the obvious the day they'd gone out for drinks and dessert. The Caribbean gingerbread she'd tasted had been marvelous with its strong flavors of molasses and ginger root; it was also sticky and spicy. Later she'd told him that he'd tricked her with plenty of wine and dessert to get her talking, when in reality, she'd been aching to release some of the tension of her situation to someone.

"You have distinct opinions," Rafe had corrected her. *"I would not call that talking too much in the general sense. You also know how to deal with people. I've watched you with Malayka."*

Oh no, Landry thought. If he'd seen her with Malayka lately, he surely thought she talked way too much, in any sense. Things hadn't really been tense between her and Malayka. They had been eye-opening. The stilted client and stylist relationship they'd had prior to Malayka's surprise appearance in her room had been shifted. Now there was a cordial coexistence. Malayka needed a stylist and she was smart enough to also realize that firing Landry would make it hard to find another stylist without answering some difficult questions. Considering she was months away from being a princess, Landry knew she would be able to hire someone in a heartbeat. Only *that someone* might not be as reputable and as well connected as Landry because news in this business spread just as rapidly as any other gossip in the life of the rich and famous. So they were at a point where Landry spoke concisely about what she knew best and Malayka either listened or risked looking half her best as a result and she did not mention Kristian or Landry's personal life again. It was a great compromise, in Landry's mind.

"I'm just trying to do my job," she'd told Rafe.

"I must admit I had never heard of such a job before. It made sense to me that people selected their own clothes, but I'm beginning to see that you do much more than that. You leave impressions on people with your words and thoughts. Your presence here in the palace has been felt," he said.

Landry hadn't known how to respond so she'd simply said, *"Thank you, sir."*

"No," he continued. *"I believe I will eventually be in a position to thank you."*

He had picked up his fork and with resignation scooped more fruit into his mouth. Landry had taken that as the end of their conversation and left the kitchen.

That had been a few days ago and now she was thinking of the prince's words as she took the last few steps leading to the ballroom entrance. It had not been her intention to attend the ball, but when she received an envelope with the royal insignia melted in red wax on the back, she'd known she was in trouble. It was an official invitation to the ball and for just a few minutes as Landry had read it, she'd felt like Cinderella.

She did not have a dress, nothing that was appropriate for a royal ball so as any other stylist worth her salt she'd slipped into a moment of panic. But just like a fairy godmother and her royal accomplice, Detali and Sam had come to the rescue.

It was after dinner last night when Landry had been toying with the idea of giving in and going for a swim that the two women had knocked on her bedroom door.

"What's this?" Sam had asked, pointing to a dress that was hanging on a rack in the sitting area.

That's where Landry had put it once she'd gone through every item of clothing she'd packed to come to the island. Sure, she could have called on one of her designer friends to ship her something quickly, but she really hadn't wanted to make a big deal out of the ball, or the fact that she was actually going to attend. She'd come to the conclusion that for her position there, the floor-length white dress with its bold pink, blue and black floral design down one side and thigh-high split on the right would be fashionable and appropriate enough. Besides, she only planned to make an appearance and then she would leave. She would not disrespect the prince by ignoring his invitation totally, but she really wasn't in the mood to act as if she were part of this world again.

Landry felt like she'd made that mistake each time she'd lain in Kristian's bed.

"I'm wearing that to the ball tomorrow," she had replied to Sam. *"Is there something wrong with Malayka's dress?"*

That question had been directed to Detali who stood quietly near the door holding a garment bag in her short arms.

"What's going on?" Landry asked when no one had answered.

"As pretty as this is, you cannot wear it tomorrow night," Sam answered then. *"Here, go try this on."*

The princess had taken the garment bag from Detali and handed it to Landry.

"What? No. My dress is fine," Landry told them.

Sam, wearing dove-gray slacks, a wide black patent leather belt and white blouse, stood in all her regal glory, giving Landry a slow shake of her head.

"It's your turn to listen when directed about fashion," Sam told her. *"Now, Detali told me she had something perfect for you and when I saw it I knew she was right. So you just go on in there and try it on. The faster you prove we also have excellent taste in gowns, the sooner you'll be able to continue closing yourself up in this room."*

A part of her had wanted to rebut Sam's statement. Not so much the part about her and Detali knowing just as much about fashion as she did, but the part about her shutting herself in this room. The smarter part of her knew that was a mistake. The last thing she wanted to do was have a conversation about her not attending dinners in the last week with Sam, in front of Detali. So with a huff she'd taken the garment bag and moments later found herself admitting that Sam and Detali had not only been right, but they'd hit the ball straight out of the park with the gown.

Royal blue—one of Landry's favorite colors—and strapless, some intricate beadwork around the bodice and cascading down to the fitted waist. It fanned out from there in a true princess cut, more of the soft blue material that ended with a sweep over the floor in an ombré style. What was really intriguing was the last six or so inches of the dress that boasted another elaborate design of darker blue over the lighter shade. When she turned, the flouncy material lifted from the floor to reveal layers of ivory material that perfectly complemented the design at the bottom.

It was gorgeous, Landry thought now as she walked toward the ballroom, the blue Manolo Blahnik Regilla pumps clicking on the glossed marble floor. The hallway was at least twenty feet wide, with its soaring ceiling and gold leaf wallpaper. Knowing that everyone else had most likely arrived at eight as the invitation had instructed, she was the lone straggler. This was, of course, due to her job and the time she'd spent getting Malayka ready. In Landry's right hand she held a royal blue satin clutch. Her left hand was clenched as she battled with nerves. When she approached the large open white-and-gold doors all the doubts that she'd tried valiantly to keep at bay these last few hours came soaring to the forefront.

She didn't belong here.

She wasn't royalty.

This was out of her league.

If her sister, Paula, could see her now she'd die with envy.

Her mother would squeal with delight at the possibility of marriage candidates in the ballroom.

Landry smiled. She missed her matchmaking mother.

She approached the two men dressed in full regalia. Thick gold tassels hung from the shoulders of their white jackets, sheathed swords on the black leather belts at their waist, black pants, shining black shoes and they had stern looks on their faces.

Landry hurriedly opened her clutch to look for the invitation, when another officially dressed man stepped from the side to take her arm.

"Allow me to escort you, Ms. Norris," he said.

"Thank you," she replied, impressed and in awe at the formality.

She shouldn't have been, at least not yet, because as Landry walked down the curved champagne-colored marble steps her breath was taken completely away at the room she was entering.

The ballroom was phenomenal. Even higher ceilings than in the hallway, this one was painted with some type of mural, golden-winged angels floating against the palest green backdrop. There was more gold adorning the walls, framing the floor-to-ceiling windows and serving as the baseboards. The floor itself was a light wood, glossed to perfection with tables along the sides leaving the entire center of the floor open.

Landry was speechless as she took the last step and looked out to the more than three hundred people in attendance. The room was full but there was more than enough space for everyone to move around. A band, complete with a harpist and violinist played a very soft melody while staff dressed in crisp white jackets and black pants moved throughout the room carrying trays of food and champagne.

A camera flash jolted Landry out of the fantasy and she looked to her right to see a small circle of photographers. Another flash and Landry looked away from them.

"There you are." She heard Roland's voice before she actually saw him since her eyes were still trying to adjust after all that flashing in her face.

"I was beginning to think you wouldn't show up," he said as he took her other arm and gave a nod to the man who had escorted her in.

When the man left, Landry walked alongside Roland. She'd never seen him this dressed up before so she couldn't help but stare.

"Ah yes, one of the few times you will see me wearing this getup," he told her with a smile. "This is how a commander in Grand Serenity's Royal Seaside Navy should dress at these prestigious events. I, on the other hand, would have loved nothing better than to throw on some jeans and a shirt and be done with it."

Landry laughed at Roland's honesty but had to admit he wore the outfit well. The white jacket with its gold buttons down the front, light blue sash crossing his chest with two gold medals dangling over was what she now recognized as the royal insignia. Another patch she presumed represented the navy's insignia.

"You look great," she told him.

"No," Roland said as he lifted her free hand to his lips to softly kiss its back. "You look fabulous."

Landry couldn't help but smile, or blush, or whatever. It felt good to be complimented and even better to be whisked so effortlessly onto the dance floor with Roland. They moved to a much slower rhythm than the music playing but Landry didn't care. Roland commented on everyone that they passed on the dance floor. From the prime minister of a neighboring island and his abysmally young, but exceptionally well-mannered new girlfriend, to the oldest member of Grand Serenity's ruling cabinet and his ongoing struggle with going bald—all his words, of course.

Landry laughed and danced and felt at ease, so much so she wouldn't have noticed anyone staring at her, not even Kristian.

She was stunning.

That was Kris's first thought as he saw her coming

down the steps. She'd looked as regal and royal as any of the wives of dignitaries who had previously walked down those same stairs. Her elbow was linked with one of the palace guard's, her head held high, a gracious smile on her face. It was as if she were meant to be here, just like everyone else.

He'd sipped slowly from the glass of champagne he'd snagged from a tray and stood close to one of the windows. It was almost an hour into the event so everyone he needed to greet had already entered. At first, Kris hadn't thought Landry was coming, because he hadn't thought to invite her.

"I'm sending the stylist an invitation," Rafe had told him on Wednesday, after the tense meeting Rafe had called where he scolded his children.

"I must say I'm shocked you hadn't already taken care of that task," his father had continued while Kris stood staring out the window of Rafe's office.

"I've had a lot to do these past few days," was Kris's eventual reply.

"I take that to mean you've met privately with your brother and sister to discuss how the three of you plan to show more respect to Malayka and our upcoming marriage," Rafe stated.

Kris had wanted to sigh. He'd still been irritated with his father's tone and directives in that regard, but once again, he hadn't argued with Rafe. While Roland had been the most vocal in the meeting, expressing his many doubts about the background story Malayka had provided, Kris had eventually calmed his brother and swore to his father that they would do better.

"We're committed to this family and our role in the royal court. We will act accordingly," he'd stiffly replied.

"She's not as bad as you believe," Rafe continued as

he reached into the dark cherry-finished humidor on his desk to retrieve a cigar.

"I'm only inclined to believe the facts," Kris had told him. *"As you've stated, that is what she's already told us about herself. So that's the end of it."*

Kris heard the flick of a lighter and even though he did not turn to look at him, he knew his father was leaning back in his leather desk chair, taking the first big puffs of his favored Cohiba Behike cigar.

"I'm not referring to Malayka," Rafe said slowly.

Kris did turn then. He remained by the window but looked directly at his father. *"I don't understand."*

Rafe took another puff and nodded. He wore a black pin-striped suit today, the jacket tossed over the back of a guest chair across the room, his white shirt crisp, and the canary-yellow tie bright. On his wrist was a gold watch that competed with the black-and-gold cuff links for spectacular gleam. On the ring finger of his right hand was the monarch ring, a thick gold band with the DeSaunters insignia on top. Kris and Roland each had one, but they only wore them on special occasions. Rafe, as the reigning prince, wore his every day.

"Do you think you're the only one who keeps tabs on things around here?" Rafe asked him. *"I know that you will someday be prince of this island, but for now, it's my job to know everything that goes on."*

"Meaning?" Kris had asked, a sense of dread growing stronger in the pit of his stomach.

"Meaning, I know that you've been spending time with that young woman."

Kris could only nod; denial would be pointless and disrespectful.

"We're both adults," was his short reply.

"You're good-looking adults. She's a spirited one. I had

the chance to speak with her alone for a bit yesterday and she was smart and polite and most of all honest. I like that about her. I suspect you did too, hence the reason you invited her to dinner with us in the first place."

Kris still didn't have a logical reason for why he'd wanted Landry at their family dinners. And he wasn't certain that he wanted to continue this conversation with his father.

"So she'll be at the ball—that's fine with me. Now, if you'll excuse me I have some calls to make," he'd said and headed toward the door.

Rafe's booming voice stopped him.

"I didn't marry royalty the first time around. I married the woman I fell madly in love with. Vivienne was intelligent and beautiful and smarter than any of the well-to-do women I'd met in my years. She was an American too, as you may recall."

Kris had inhaled deeply, exhaled slowly and turned to face his father once more.

"I know who and what my mother was," he spoke quietly.

Rafe took another drag from his cigar before setting it in the ashtray. Puffs of smoke haloed around him and when the smoke cleared Kris could see his father staring directly at him.

"Then I'm sure you also know how she felt about building a life around love. Vivienne would never let the title, this palace or anything else come between herself and love. She expected nothing less of her children."

Kris clenched his teeth, but did not let out the sigh he wished to. *"I don't know what you're trying to say, Dad."*

"Yes, you do, son. You're just trying to deny it. You're trying to convince yourself that you're doing the noble thing by staying strong and keeping up the pretense. What you don't realize is that it's not what you say or what you

even acknowledge publicly, Kris. Your feelings are in the way you look at her, the tension that immediately bubbles inside of you when someone else speaks of her. You went to eat pizza with her and frolicked in the water with her. You haven't eaten pizza since your sister was young."

"It was just pizza."

Rafe chuckled then, a deep, full-bodied laughter that filled the entire room.

"It was the beginning," Rafe told him finally. *"And the ending will be what you make it. Remember that, Kris."*

Kris had forgotten the conversation with his father almost immediately as he'd returned to his office to see a message from someone he needed desperately to speak to. He handled the call, made private travel arrangements and then thought about what his father had said. He was responsible for the ending. Landry had said something similar that night in the garden.

"You create your own circumstances, control your own destiny. It doesn't have to be prewritten. Unless you want it to be," she'd said. The way she'd looked at him had been brutally honest because she believed every word of it.

She and his father obviously believed more than he did.

Kris wondered if they were both right. Landry had walked away from him that night in the garden. She'd asked him not to contact her again and he'd done as she'd requested because he understood why she needed it to stop. The real truth was he hadn't thought he had the strength to stop their affair himself; his need for her seemed so urgent and unceasing. Yet, she'd done it. She'd said the words and she'd meant them. He admired her for that.

He admired her and he hated seeing her in Roland's arms, all at the same time.

They were dancing close together, Roland's hand was around her waist, the other holding her hand. He'd even bent forward and kissed her forehead. Kris's fingers tightened on the stem of the champagne glass.

"Looks like Roland is stealing your woman," Sam said as she came to stand beside him.

Once again, he was prepared to deny the way he felt, but he had been staring at Landry and thinking about her, and dammit, his father must have been right.

"I've seen the way you look at her and I saw the pictures of you and her at the museum in the paper. While the island is speculating, I know firsthand how different you've been behaving since she's been here."

Kris finished off the champagne and immediately looked for a place to dispose of the glass. Catching the eye of one of the staff members, he waited until the man came over and took the glass from him, before replying to his sister.

It was a stall tactic, but one Kris desperately needed. He'd seen the papers as well so he knew what was being said after he'd taken Landry to the opening ceremony of the new exhibit at the museum two weeks ago. It had been an impromptu invitation. He'd fully intended to go alone, as usual. But then he'd thought about her and before he could stop himself he'd gone to her room and made the request. She'd looked hopeful and he knew it. The moment he'd asked her to accompany him, she'd thought it was a date. It wasn't; it was business and he'd been sure to make that known. After explaining that to her, he hadn't touched her or stood too close to her at all during the ceremony and when it was done, he hadn't even offered her dinner, instead telling Tajeo to bring them straight home.

It wasn't a date. He wasn't courting her.

They were just…just…

"Just how do you think I've been behaving? I haven't done anything out of the ordinary," he replied to Sam, even though he knew deep down how big of a lie his words actually were.

"For one, you took her to the museum unveiling and that was after you insisted that she be at the family dinners. You're also keeping tabs of her comings and goings with Jorge."

"As you well know, I'm concerned about everyone riding in our cars now, so that doesn't count."

"You let Jorge pick her up from the front of the palace when everyone else leaves from the back. I know you know about this and you must have approved it or Jorge would not be doing it."

"I'm just concerned for her safety, like everyone else here."

"Yeah right, Kris, tell that to the reporters—they might believe you. But I certainly don't. You've been staring at her since she walked into this room and now that Roland's got his arms—very tightly I might add—around her, you're about to explode with jealousy."

Kris forced himself to look away from where Landry and Roland were; just as Sam said, they were dancing very closely together. He wished for another glass of champagne but knew that it wouldn't look good for him to be seen drinking too many. "I'm not jealous."

Sam was nodding when he looked in her direction. "No, you're not stupid," she told him, "which is what I would have to call you if you stood here like a silly oaf instead of going over there and interrupting their dance. If you want something in life, Kris, you've just got to go out there and grab hold of it with both hands."

He frowned at her then. "Mom used to say that."

"She sure did," Sam admitted. "And it's never been truer than it is now. So get yourself out there and grab what you want."

Kris wasn't taking advice from his younger sister. Nor was he heeding his father's words. He was simply going to ask her to dance with him. It was polite and it would also keep him from having to dance with anyone else, at least for the moment. So he walked out onto the dance floor, excusing himself through the crowd as others danced around him.

Just as he was close enough to them to tap Roland on the back, another woman appeared with a smile.

"Good evening, Your Highness," she said before falling into a deep curtsy, her gaze going from him to Roland and back to him.

Roland had stopped dancing but still held Landry in his arms.

"Well, look what we have here," Roland said with his signature grin in place. "A situation."

Landry looked up to Kris and let her hands fall slowly from Roland's shoulders.

"I believe introductions are necessary," Kris said.

"Yes, they certainly are. Please, let me, big brother," Roland added with a wink.

Kris resisted the urge to frown.

"Landry Norris, this is Valora Harrington," Roland began with a flourish of his arm between the two ladies. "Valora, this is Landry. She's a guest to the palace and is assisting Malayka in preparations for the wedding."

Valora nodded, her short dark hair an intriguing contrast to her buttery skin tone.

"It's a pleasure to meet you," Valora said. "I read in the paper how you've been visiting the local dressmakers. They have wonderful things to say about you."

Landry accepted the hand that Valora extended and smiled in return. "Thanks. I'm happy to meet you as well. As for the dressmakers, there's an amazing amount of talent on this island. I just hope to be able to share it with those in my country soon."

"Of course you will," Roland quipped. "Especially since the gowns you and Malayka are both wearing tonight are made by Detali."

Kris had no idea how his brother knew that, since he obviously had no clue, but he found that he was pleased by the knowledge.

"Your gown is beautiful," Landry said to Valora.

Valora smiled and accepted the compliment but Kris was certain something else was going on there. He could feel the edges of tension and wondered for a moment if it were solely due to his presence.

"Well, Valora. Why don't we take a spin on this grand dance floor," Roland offered. "Kris, you dance with Landry."

Before he could say a word—even though he fully planned to agree with Roland's suggestion—Roland had taken Valora's hand and they were walking away. Kris didn't wait for Landry to respond, he simply stepped in front of her and took her hand. He held her just as Roland had, except their bodies were not nearly as close. They moved slowly, almost mechanically in the same spot.

After a few quiet moments, she sighed.

"You don't have to do this," she told him. "I understand if you wanted to dance with Valora. I mean, I know that you two aren't actually engaged. Roland told me. But still, I get if you'd rather be seen with a native, instead of with me."

"What's that supposed to mean? And how did you find out about me and Valora?" Kris asked as they continued to move.

She looked away, then back to him like she was really considering walking away and leaving him alone on the dance floor. He was thankful when she let out a sigh but looked as if she'd stay.

"Malayka told me you were engaged," she admitted.

"When did she tell you that? Is that why you ended things between us?"

"What?" she asked, surprise clearly on her face. "No. She didn't tell me until after I'd done that. I said we could no longer do what we were doing because it was wrong, for both of us."

"You cannot speak for me," he said. He was getting really tired of people telling him what he felt, and how he should react to what he felt.

"No, but I can speak for what I was involved in. We both knew it was pointless from the start," she said and still would not look directly at him.

She blinked when a camera flashed close to them. On the other side, another flash went off and this time Kris was the one blinking.

"Great," she said with a sigh. "Now they're going to print in the paper that you were dancing with the American stylist. Perhaps they'll say you took pity on me or some other nonsense."

"They've already snapped pictures of us and I would demand a retraction if they dared to insult you in any way," he told her as he looked over her head for one of the guards.

When he saw a familiar face and they exchanged a look, Kris relaxed a bit. But that was short-lived.

"There you are," Malayka said tightly as she came behind Landry to take hold of her arm. "I've been looking everywhere for you. It seems I'm having a wardrobe malfunction."

"Oh no, really? Did something happen to the dress?"

"Something happened alright. A reporter just asked me about my Detali original. I wasn't aware that I was wearing a Detali original, or who the hell Detali is for that matter," Malayka argued.

Kris was just about to say something when Landry shook her head at him. "I can handle this on my own. Let's go," she told Malayka and they walked away.

The cameramen had just taken a flurry of new shots and Kris could imagine what the headline would read.

Soon-to-Be Princess Argues with Crown Prince's Mistress.

He clenched his fists at the thought.

"Hey, we can go over those reports first thing tomorrow. I think I've found something interesting," Gary said after he and another guard had moved the photographers along.

"Sure," Kris said as he looked around the ballroom to see if he could catch a glimpse of the direction Malayka and Landry had headed.

He wasn't comfortable with Malayka's tone and felt like he needed to be close just in case.

Then suddenly noise became deafening. The floor and the walls shook, smoke filled the air instantly and screaming immediately followed.

Chapter 14

Pandemonium quickly ensued as smoke and flames filled the back portion of the ballroom.

Garrison "Gary" Montgomery, Kris's college friend who also happened to be a former captain in the United States Army, had just come to stand by Kris and immediately pushed him to the floor, using his body to cover Kris as the explosion rocked the room.

"You okay?" he'd asked almost immediately.

Kris nodded. "I'm good. Find my father!"

By that point he was getting to his feet and then he was looking around. People were still screaming and running around, falling over each other. Kris instantly began moving. He did not run, but walked quickly, touching people as he went so that he could move by them without knocking them down. When he saw a guard he grabbed the man's arm.

"Get all guards down here. Call the police and the paramedics and find my sister and brother, now!"

The guard took off in another direction and Kris continued to move. Until he stopped to help an elderly woman who had either fallen or had simply sat on the steps, one hand clutching her chest, the other one shaking as she tried to hold on to the railing.

"Ma'am, it's best if we get you out of here," he told her and slipped his arms beneath her to hoist her up off the floor.

She was shaking her head, tears streaming down her face as she said, "My Carl, my husband. I don't know where he is."

Kris nodded. "We'll find him. But he would want you to get to safety. I'm going to help you get out of here."

After another wail she wrapped her arms tightly around Kris's neck leaned into him as he led them around the stairs to another door.

This was the staff hallway, which they used to get to and from the kitchen quickly. Kris walked her through the passageway where there were still people, but a smaller amount since nobody really knew about that area but the staff. When he came to a back door that led out to the side of the palace, he used his foot to kick it open and then hurried through with the woman.

They both inhaled the fresh evening air, sucking in gulps and coughing a little from the smoke that had already began to fill their lungs. Uniformed guards were coming from around the front of the house and Kris waved one of them down.

"Get her out of here," he told the guard. "And find her husband, Carl."

When Kris turned to go back inside, the guard protested.

"Your Highness, you should come this way. We're clearing everyone from the palace," he told Kris.

Kris only nodded. "That's good. Get everyone out. Get them all out and hurry!"

He then walked past the guard, through the door and ran down the hallway. In seconds he was in the ballroom once again. Lifting his jacket to cover his mouth and nose Kris proceeded through the crowd, yelling at them to keep moving to the exits as fast as they could. At the same time he came to another door, the one that he knew was a back stairwell leading up to the second floor. This was where he'd seen Malayka and Landry go only seconds before the explosion.

Kris took the steps two at a time, stopping only when he came to another door which he yanked open. Running down that hallway he let his jacket fall from his face because there was no visible smoke there. This side of the floor housed conference rooms and the room Kris knew that Malayka was now using as a dressing room. That's where they had to be.

He wasn't certain they'd had enough time to actually reach the room but Kris ran in that direction anyway, until he saw her lying on the floor. With fear threatening to choke him, Kris ran faster until his feet were skidding across the floor as he tried to stop. Dropping to his knees he lifted her head and let it rest on his arm as he called her name.

"Landry! Landry! Talk to me!"

He wanted to smack her face to wake her but was too afraid of further hurting her. Instead he grabbed her cheeks between his fingers, shaking her as gingerly as his trembling hands could manage.

"Landry!"

Her eyes fluttered after a few seconds then opened again slowly, her lips parting.

"What did you hit me with?" she asked groggily.

"Not me, baby. Never. I would never hurt you. Ever."

But somebody had.

Somebody had hit Landry and set off an explosive in his house.

"Everybody is accounted for," Roland said as he entered the room about half an hour after the explosion. "Malayka is in her room resting, per your orders. And I stopped by Sam's room before coming back here. She's more pissed off than afraid, but there are four guards with her."

Kris watched as his brother gave a nod to their father and then crossed the carpeted floor, stopping at the end of a leather couch to sit on its wide arm. His jacket was gone, the white T-shirt he'd worn beneath it smudged with dark marks. Rafe sat in a wide, cushioned chair, an unlit cigar between his fingers.

The moment a guard had found him to tell him where his family was Kris had stood, knowing he needed to go to them. He'd taken Landry to her room by then and she'd sat on the sofa, her still-shaking hands holding a glass of water. Another guard had seen Kris bring her in there and immediately offered his assistance. Kris instructed the guard to stay with Landry and had given her one long last look, as she sat huddled beneath his black commander's jacket, which he'd wrapped around her shoulders.

She was alive.

He breathed a sigh of relief and went to make sure the rest of his family were fine as well. They were all accounted for, and all pissed off.

"Brakes have been tampered with, someone broke into the bank and now this," Roland said, the tension in his voice filtering throughout the room. "An explosion at the palace. Who the hell is behind this?"

Roland had shouted the question, displaying the fury

that was no doubt going through each of them. They were in his father's private rooms. Kris stood close to the bar but hadn't allowed himself to fix a drink. They could all probably use one, but he refrained because he wanted his mind to be perfectly clear when the police arrived.

As if he'd silently summoned them, there was a soft knock on the door. Roland stood and walked the length of the floor to answer it. They came in, Salvin leading the way, followed by Captain Vincent Briggins, head of the Grand Serenity Police Force, and Garrison Montgomery. As Roland closed the door and followed the men, Kris walked over to stand near them.

"Let me introduce Garrison Montgomery—he's a retired captain in the United States Army and a personal friend of mine," Kris told them.

"Should he be here right now?" Roland asked.

Kris nodded to his brother. "He's the security expert I hired after our conversation."

The look he was giving Roland was pointed and meant to convey the rest of the statement Kris did not want his father to hear. Instead of paying the exorbitant amount of money and giving in to the ridiculous demands of Roland's associate Yiker, Kris had decided to go another route. Roland nodded his understanding but Kris was certain they'd have a more in-depth conversation about it later.

"What have you found? Who did this?" Rafe asked by way of dismissing whatever else Kris and Roland may have wanted to say.

"It was a small device, very amateurish and working on a remote detonator that was left on the balcony. That's why the major impact was in the back of the ballroom," Salvin began.

"What about injuries? Fatalities?" Kris asked.

Captain Briggins shook his head. "There were two fatalities, Your Highness. They were standing closest to the doors. Other guests were either on the dance floor or seated at their table—this put them at a farther distance from the impact. There are injuries and the last time I checked in, ambulances were circling back from the hospital to transport them all. If it had been a better-built bomb, using more reliable explosives, the fatalities and damages would no doubt be far worse."

Grand Serenity had a population of just over one hundred thousand citizens. There were two hospitals, one on each side of the island, and approximately twelve ambulances. Kris had presumed there would be a large number of injuries, but he hadn't wanted to accept fatalities. He frowned.

"I want to know what is going on here!" Rafe roared.

"If I may be permitted to speak," Gary interjected.

Kris nodded. "Please. This is a closed conversation—what you say here will go no further than this room."

Gary nodded. "First, everyone, please call me Gary. I've been on the island for just a few days, but from what I can tell this is a beautiful place." He cleared his throat. "Except for the circumstances that brought me here."

"Kris called you so I'm assuming there's a need for an outside security expert," Rafe said in response to Gary.

"Yes, I've been looking into each of the incidents that have happened. My investigation is nowhere near complete but as I told Kris before the explosion, I may have found something interesting."

"What is it?" Roland asked.

Gary looked to Kris and then folded his arms over his chest as he began again. "One of the first things I noticed was that these incidents all began after a certain time. Prince Rafferty, you've been seeing Malayka Sampson since late February."

Rafe straightened. "That is correct," he said in a voice that told everyone in the room that he wasn't going to take kindly to anything said against Malayka.

Gary kept talking. Whether or not he was moved to omit anything because of Rafe's tone was something Kris would find out later.

"She first visited the palace in March," Gary continued. "You traveled for three weeks in April and then you returned to the palace alone."

"Yes," Rafe said, coming to his feet now. "She went back to the States to pack her things. I moved her into the palace the first of May, after I proposed to her."

Gary nodded.

"She moved in and then she returned to the States briefly."

"To attend some function she was already committed to," Rafe replied.

"Yes," Gary said. "The Met Gala. Then the second week of May she returned, this time someone came with her."

Kris tensed as he said tightly, "Landry."

Another nod from Gary, this time in Kris's direction.

"The car accident happened in late May, the break-in at the bank—"

"The one nobody thought was important enough to tell me about," Rafe interrupted.

Kris picked up with the story then, the words raspy to his ears. "The break-in occurred in late June."

Almost one month after he'd begun sleeping with Landry.

"I invited her to the ball," Rafe whispered and then shook his head. "Wait a minute—you're not seriously suggesting what I think you are? Landry Norris, the stylist? You really think she's involved in this."

"She's a common denominator," Gary offered.

"She has nothing to gain," Roland added.

"How do we know this?" Rafe asked. "Who is she connected to? Wasn't she thoroughly investigated like anyone else staying at the palace?"

"Yes," Kris answered emphatically. "I did an extensive background check before she came to the island and then I interviewed her when she arrived."

He remembered how pretty she'd looked in that fitted skirt and how nervous he'd thought she was even though she seemed calm. He also recalled the seconds that had ticked by as he'd contemplated kissing her before Sam had interrupted them.

"I don't believe it," Roland said instantly. "She wouldn't do this. She cares about the people here. She went against Malayka in order to bring Detali's talents to the forefront. She wouldn't have done that if she had something against us, our country. There has to be another scenario."

"Where was she when the explosion occurred?" Gary asked.

All eyes fell to Kris.

"We were dancing and then…" He didn't get a chance to finish his statement before the door opened and in a blur of blue material, Landry came bustling in.

"Oh my God! I heard them planning this! I heard them the other day!" she said as she came to a stop in front of him. "I heard it all!"

Landry had been sitting in that room with her head throbbing, trying her best to remember what had happened.

One minute she was dancing with Roland, laughing and joking with him the same way she used to with her brothers back home. The next, she was with Kristian, hating that it felt so good to be in his arms again, when she knew that it wouldn't last. Then, Malayka wanted to speak to her.

From that point on, her memory was foggy, until he was there again, and she was in his arms…again.

Damn, she loved how he smelled. It was unlike any cologne she'd ever known. He'd looked dashing and desirable, in his dark jacket lined with more medals than Roland's, but the same light blue sash crossing his chest. His pants were black too, which gave him an even more debonair appearance. His jaw was strong and tense, as usual, his dark eyes shooting fiery pinpricks in her direction.

Then there was pain and he was carrying her and she was wearing his jacket. He'd left her alone but his scent had remained.

"Saturday," Landry said when she realized Kristian was looking at her as if she'd lost her mind.

Her hair was probably a mess. She'd had an ice pack smashed against the side of it for who knew how long.

"When I walked into the room…um, Malayka's new fitting room. He was in the room next door, or the balcony, I mean," she continued.

"Who was?" Roland asked.

Landry turned and the room also picked that moment to do this spinning thing and she instantly felt nauseous. Kristian was quick. His strong arm wrapping around her waist as he held her up.

"She needs to see a doctor," Kristian shouted. "She's hurt."

"Call for the paramedics to come up here."

She heard another voice say, but Landry couldn't figure out who it belonged to. She was on another couch, Kristian right beside her now. Her head felt as if someone were pounding it with their fists and she wasn't sure how much longer she'd be able to resist the nausea.

"Who did you hear speaking?"

The question came from Prince Rafe; she knew his voice. Turning much slower this time, Landry looked at him.

"I don't know who he is, but he was on the phone telling someone to follow his orders. He kept saying nine o'clock," Landry told them.

"The explosion was at nine-oh-one."

This statement came from another man who was dressed in an official law officer uniform. Two other men that she did not know were also present. The one dressed in a simple gray suit was looking from her to Kristian as if he wanted to say something.

"He was in the house," Roland said. "Someone that works for us planned this."

"I want a list of all the staff on my desk within the hour. Check the palace once more and then lock her down tight. Nobody goes in or out without me knowing," Prince Rafe directed.

The other official-looking guy nodded and hurried out of the room.

"Who else overheard this conversation?"

This question came from the guy in the gray suit. Landry did not know who he was but if he were in this room with Kristian and the rest of the royal family, he must have been important and privy to this discussion.

"Nobody," she answered. "Malayka was late for the meeting. I was there on time and when I entered the room, there was no one else in there. The balcony doors were open and I could hear the voices. I stepped outside for just a second and that's when I saw him on the phone. He was also talking to someone in the room, but I couldn't see that person."

"So you heard this conversation and you never thought to say anything to anyone about it?" Gray-Suit-Guy asked her.

Landry wasn't sure but his question sounded a bit accusatory. But maybe she had a concussion and was confusing things.

"I didn't think to tell anyone. I don't normally eavesdrop and then tell what I've heard," she replied.

"You didn't think that you should share that someone was going to plant a bomb at the ball?" the remaining official-looking guy asked. "And then you were mysteriously not in the ballroom when the bomb went off."

"What?" she asked and pressed her hand to her stomach in an effort to cease the rolling sensation. "Malayka needed something…she wanted to…her dress." Landry took a slow breath and released it. "Wait, you think I… that I knew?"

"We would like to question you further," the official guy said.

"Me?" Landry asked.

She looked around the room to see that all eyes were on her. Then she turned to him. Kristian was staring at her as well. He wasn't saying a word. He wasn't defending her.

The battle was lost.

She jumped up off the couch and ran to the first door she saw and went inside. Luckily it was a bathroom and fortunately she'd made it in time.

Chapter 15

The room was dark and cool. After lying still for a few moments Landry realized that a steady breeze was coming through the windows. No, she thought when she chanced moving slowly to lie on her side, it was coming from the balcony.

She'd opened her eyes and blinked a few times to clear her vision. She still felt drowsy as she once again tried to recall where she was and how she'd come to be there. After noticing that she must've kicked the blankets off while she slept and that she was just a little chilly, she also realized that this wasn't her room.

Landry took her time sitting up. It was slow going because her body felt ten times heavier than usual to move. However, fortunately, she was not experiencing any pain. There had been pain before, she recalled. Intense pain… she lifted a hand to gingerly touch the bandage on her head. It was wrapped all the way around, her hair matted to the sides. Dropping her hands down with a sigh she looked around at her surroundings. A dresser, a picture, anything that would tell her where she was. But she picked up on nothing but the scent.

She was in Kristian's room.

Her location immediately alarmed her because the memory of their last conversation came flooding back.

The DeSaunters family thought she'd planted a bomb in their house. She'd never messed up this big before. Even though she hadn't planted a bomb, so technically this wasn't her mess-up. The sooner she made that point clear, the better she would feel about the rest, which she definitely did not feel like thinking about right now.

Landry took her time climbing out of the bed, stepping down from the bed's platform with careful movements. She was wearing a nightgown that did not belong to her, yet it fit her perfectly. On bare feet she relied on her memory of the space to guide her to the balcony where she figured he had to be because of the persistent breeze from the doors being open. She paused when she stepped outside to find him standing at the railing.

His balcony was much bigger than the one attached to her room, wrapping around to meet the living-room side of his private space. There were chairs and two tables in the area she could see. The air was tinged with the tropical surroundings, a scent she'd come to love in the almost two months that she'd been there. And the man, well, his broad back and opposing silhouette fit perfectly against the backdrop of endless sky and dark, ominous sea.

"You should be asleep," he said without turning around.

Landry didn't want to be comfortable. She wanted to say what she needed to say and then attempt to go back to her room. She wasn't certain what time it was, but she knew she did not want to wake up in Kristian's room come sunrise. But she needed to make sure he knew she was innocent before going back to her rooms, and possibly back home.

"I get the feeling I've slept for long enough," she replied. "How long has it been?"

"About five hours," he responded, still keeping his back to her.

That didn't bother Landry, or she convinced herself that it didn't. She wasn't sure how she would feel if he looked her in the eye and admitted he thought she could do something like this to his family. Not to mention all the innocent people that had been in that ballroom.

"I told you the truth," she began. "As soon as I realized what I'd heard meant something, I came to tell you. The guard hadn't wanted me to move because the paramedics hadn't come to see me yet. He was even more nervous about helping me find your father's private rooms, but I sort of threatened to scream throughout the entire palace if he didn't assist."

Kristian shook his head. "We need better-trained guards."

Landry took in a shaky breath and released it slowly.

"I didn't think about what I'd heard until last night as I was trying to figure out what happened. If for one moment I'd thought that it meant something before, I would have certainly told you," she continued.

"Even though you've made yourself scarce this past week?" he asked.

She sighed and folded her arms over her chest.

"It's been a busy week trying to ensure Malayka was ready for the ball."

"You had dinner in your room or you went out visiting several restaurants in town," he said.

"You know where I went?"

"Each time you left the palace, I knew. The press did as well. After seeing us together at the museum, they've taken an interest in you." His hands gripped the railing and he leaned over it slightly.

He was wearing sweatpants and a T-shirt. His appearance shocked her momentarily because she'd only ever seen Kristian in dress clothes.

"I can't believe you were keeping tabs on me," she said, baffled. "You never trusted me, did you?"

He was quiet a few seconds. "It's my job to know everything that goes on here."

"Was it your job to sleep with me too? If so, you did a good job of it. For four weeks, it was a phenomenal experience," Landry stated, her throat a little dry with the words.

No response came from him.

"Well, I only wanted to tell you that I did not… I would have never planned to set off a bomb in your home. I don't know who that man was or who he was speaking to on the phone or in the other room. I'm not even sure how I received this gash on my head. What I do know is that I'm a professional. I'm good at my job and that's why I was asked to come here. Everything else, what happened between us, I mean, well, that wasn't planned."

She could hear the sound of the sea below and a chill ran through her body. She rubbed her arms.

"So that's all. I'll go back to my room now and I'll speak with Malayka in the morning about finding her another stylist."

Kris remained silent and Landry turned to walk back into the room. She presumed he would let her go, just as he had that night in the garden. He would not talk about this, or anything, for that matter, beyond the few words he'd decided were enough. She'd come to expect nothing more from him. The Crown Prince Kristian DeSaunters was a man of few words, very minimal explanations and no regrets. He was stern in his beliefs, loyal to a fault and the only man to ever have Landry doubt herself. For that, she hated him.

"I made her a promise," he said, his voice so low she almost didn't hear him.

Landry stopped, but this time, she was the one with her back facing him.

"*Promise me you'll be good, Kris.* That's what she'd said. I stood at the side of her bed in that hospital room and she reached her hand out to me. I didn't want to touch it because there was a needle taped down on the back of it. The room smelled funny, sterile and medicinal. *Promise me you'll make your father and me proud*, she'd continued. I took her hand, twining my fingers with hers the way we used to do when I was younger and we went for walks along the beach. I told her I would be good and that I would rule this island the way she and my father expected me to. I promised her."

Landry shivered once more, but this time it wasn't because she was cold. His words were seeping inside of her, creeping into that door she'd vowed to keep closed off to him after the night in the garden.

"After that she told me she loved me. No matter what title I held or how beautiful this palace was, she loved me because I was her son," he said and Landry heard his voice crack on his last word.

There was a quick pause and he continued, "I was her son and I killed her."

Landry turned then, almost too fast as her legs threatened to buckle. Extending an arm, she grabbed hold of the back of a chair that was thankfully close.

"You did what?" she asked.

Kristian turned then as well. He leaned against the railing in a move that looked so casual and so enticing. At another time it might have drawn her closer to him; tonight, it kept her still.

"She loved to ride horses," he began. "We have a stable…we *used* to have a stable down farther to the west side of the palace. She would ride in the hills and then take her horse, Trolly, down to the beach to cool down. I didn't like to ride. Sam did. She loved it as much as my mother. They loved to do a lot of things together."

He looked off to the side, then back to her.

"Sam was her little girl and Roland was her sunshine. I was her constant. She used to say that she knew what I would do and say before I did because I was constantly trying to be an adult. She was right. Instead of riding with her, I watched her ride and when she was finished I took care of the horse and locked up the stable. I was ten years old and one day, that day, I'd been reading a book instead of watching her ride.

"I knew she was out there and I'd come to sit on the cliff to watch her, but I brought a book with me. One my father would have flipped if he saw me with."

"Which book?" Landry asked even though she was sure that wasn't the most important part of this story.

"Romeo and Juliet," he said with a shrug. "I found it in my mother's library. She'd had a bookmark in it so I knew she'd read it. That enticed me to read it too."

"I read it for the first time when I was in the tenth grade," Landry admitted. "I've read it at least a dozen times since then."

"I was so into the book that I almost missed the fact that she'd finished her ride and was coming back to the stables. I had to run to get there in time. She was already wiping the horse down and feeding him carrots. She smiled when she saw me and said it was okay that I hadn't been here, that she could take care of it. I didn't like seeing her doing my job." He sighed. "So I put the book down and I insisted on finishing up for her. There was a storm coming and she said we needed to batten everything down tightly. I agreed. And I thought I'd done that."

He dragged his hands down his face and shook his head. "The storm hit later that evening. We had just finished dinner and one of the staff came in to say that they were being called down to the stables. My mother insisted on going down. My father stood to go with her but I told him I would go instead."

"Because that was your job," Landry said. "You weren't old enough to rule the island yet, but you still had responsibilities."

He nodded. "I went out with her and two of the staff. When we got there the stable doors were swinging in the gusty wind. My mother instantly ran toward the stable. I ran behind her but I tripped over something. I still don't know what, but in the few seconds it took for me to get up and start forward again, Trolly had gotten loose from his stall. He'd barreled through, knocking my mother down. She hit her head on the stall door and only regained consciousness for a half hour before she died."

Landry's hands shook as tears filled her eyes. The sorrow in his tone was heart-wrenching; the rush of realizations and unspoken explanations bombarded her with sadness.

"It wasn't your fault," she said immediately.

"I must've failed to lock the stall doors."

"What if the wind was simply so strong it blew them open?" she insisted.

"I should have bolted them. We knew the storm was coming and it was my responsibility. I was next in line to be leader. How could I lead effectively if I forgot something so simple?"

"Oh, Kristian," she sighed.

He shook his head again as if the act was meant to shake away any pity she might have felt for him. To make his point clearer, he stood straight and took a step toward her.

"I am the next in line to rule. Everything that happens here is ultimately my responsibility. If you were a threat to us, I should have known. But how could I if I were so busy falling...falling into bed with you like some lust-filled schoolboy," he said.

The words stung and Landry struggled to remain standing.

"I should have remained focused. I should have brought Gary in sooner to look things over. That's my job!" he yelled.

Landry jumped at the spike in his voice.

"You couldn't control our attraction any more than I could," she told him. "So no, you can't add that to your list of failures. You and I both decided to sleep together. And don't think you're the only one who had doubts about that because I did too."

A renewed energy surged through her. Maybe it was the anger she'd begun to feel when he spoke like he finally regretted something else in his life, which was sleeping with her.

"Do you think I wanted to come here and get so caught up in a guy, not to mention a prince of all people in this world? I've fought tooth and nail with my parents over submitting to a man, over giving parts of myself to someone, parts that I cherished. After that first night all you had to do was send me a text and I came running. The day you invited me to the museum with you I was elated because I thought it was a real date. We weren't only sleeping together, we were dating. For a moment, one brief second in time, I entertained the idea of us becoming a real couple.

"Do you know what that meant to me? No, you don't. But you probably figure I'm like Malayka and it meant some type of power trip, or possibly that I was enamored by your riches and this island and all that went with the title of being princess. But you would be so very wrong. I never wanted marriage and a happy-ever-after and I certainly never wanted that with a prince!"

Her entire body was shaking with rage now. She wanted to cry and to scream. A part of her ached for him, for that ten-year-old boy who had lost his mother and covered himself in blame for an accident that should not have been his responsibility to control. And another part wanted to punch him in the face for being so callous with her and what they'd shared.

"But you know what, Your Highness? I'm a big enough person that I can admit my faults and accept when I've made a mistake. I came to you willingly. I should have known better. I did actually, but I ignored the warnings. I did what I always do and took a leap. Now I'll deal with the fact that I was wrong about you. I thought you were strong and admirable, but I should have known you were just another conceited jerk believing in your own self-importance more than you actually believed in yourself."

Her heart was thumping, her arms were chilled as she stood there squaring off with him. He looked like he was ready to explode, as if he had so much more he could but of course would not say to her. Landry realized at that point that she didn't give a damn. Whatever else Kristian wanted to say to her, she just didn't care. Not anymore.

"I'm going back to my room now and I'm going to pack my things. I'll be out of here by tomorrow morning. Investigate me some more if you still think I slept with you just so I could plant a bomb in the palace and possibly kill you and your family. Do whatever you have to do."

Landry prayed she wouldn't pass out as he moved. The perfect ending to this scene was her walking out with her head held high. She managed it, on bare feet and wearing a silky nightgown. When she finally arrived at her room she slammed the door shut and slid to the floor where she sat. She cried and then finally, she picked herself up and began to pack, determined to move forward, just as she always had.

In the morning Kris had received word that Landry was gone; he was still sitting on the balcony when Sam came in.

"I heard about what happened while I was safely tucked in my room last night. I won't tell you how big of a jerk you are because you're my brother and I love you," she said as she sat on one of the lounge chairs beside him. "But wow, you are a jerk!"

Kris leaned forward, resting his elbows on his knees.

"I don't need you to tell me what I already know," he said.

How many times had he had that very thought in the hours that he'd been out here?

"She didn't do this," Sam said.

"I know."

"She's gone."

He tried not to react too much to those words.

"I know."

"You're in love with her," Sam continued.

"I'm no good for her," he replied.

Sam chuckled. "That's such a sorry cop-out. And you're too smart to say things like that."

Kris agreed. He was smart. He'd always performed well in school and had done even better in college. He was ambitious and tenacious. He'd been trained to be a pillar of strength in the midst of any adversity. He could negotiate with the best businessmen but always kept his eye on his bottom line. He was not a lover and had never dealt with any relationship issues, ever. So yeah, he guessed that gave him a pass to say some things that weren't so smart, at least once in his life.

"I wasn't smart enough to handle the situation better," he admitted.

"Well, inexperience has to count for something," Sam said.

Trust his younger sister to be the one dishing out words of wisdom. Whenever he and Roland used to argue Sam would come along with one of her many dolls in tow and mediate with such calm maturity Kris had often wondered if she were really meant to be the oldest.

"It doesn't matter," he told her. "I have to deal with whoever is trying to kill us, or Dad, or whatever is going on here." Dragging his hands over his face he came to stand. "I've got to shower and meet with Dad and the guards. We have to get to the bottom of this."

Sam waved a hand. "Dad and Roland have been in a closed-door meeting with the guards and the police chief for the past hour."

"Why didn't they call me? I've been up. If there was going to be a meeting I should have been there," he argued.

"From what Roland told me, you carried Landry down to the health suite. Then you insisted on bringing her up to your room after the doctor had examined her and given her pain medication. He presumed you would not want to be disturbed this morning. I, on the other hand, went to check on Landry in her rooms where I thought she would be. Imagine my surprise to see her packing."

He dismissed the image of Landry packing to leave

from his mind. "This is my house, my job!" Kris insisted. He cursed and headed for the door.

"That's not all there is to your life, Kris," Sam said.

She'd stood as well and now had her hands perched on her hips. The stance and her words reminded him instantly of their mother and Kris swallowed hard to keep the grief at bay.

"Nobody doubts that you're a good leader, you've been tossing that in mine and Roland's faces all our lives. You're Dad's right hand. You know more about the banks than he does. And your birth rank overrules any argument about who will rule next. But, Kris, you've got to live too. Go bike riding, jet skiing, try sky diving, something! Get out of this palace and live a little. The title and all that goes with it will still be here and it'll still be yours."

He sighed heavily and walked to her then. He didn't do this often and he knew he probably should, but Kris pulled Sam in close for a hug. He kissed the top of her head and whispered, "I don't know if I should be leading this country if my baby sister is so much smarter than I am."

She'd wrapped her arms around his waist and laughed. "I won't tell if you don't."

Chapter 16

Two Weeks Later

Astelle took the long fork she had been using to hold the ham in place while she sliced it to poke Heinz lightly on the arm. He was trying to steal a slice and she had to remind him in a gentle tone, "The ham is not for you. There's a pan of baked chicken right there."

With a frown Heinz pulled his arm back. He then reached over to the pan of baked chicken and used his fork to pick up a thigh.

"You'll love it, Dad," Landry said, leaning over to whisper in her father's ear. "I had some of the spices I picked up in Grand Serenity shipped here and when Mom wasn't looking I sprinkled a bit on the thighs and legs because I know they're your favorite."

Heinz smiled at his daughter. "That's my girl."

"I thought I was your girl, PopPop," Giselle, Landry's

sister Paula's four-year-old, said after taking a bite of her corn on the cob.

Her niece's plump cheeks now displayed bits of corn as she chewed earnestly. Landry smiled and picked up a napkin to wipe her face.

"You're my special baby girl," Heinz told her and promptly leaned down to plant a kiss on her newly cleaned cheek.

"Spoiled rotten," Astelle said after slicing the last bit of ham and taking a seat. "Every girl child in this household has been spoiled to the point of no return."

"Tell me about it," Heinz Jr. remarked.

"That is so not true," Landry added. "How many times did the boys get out of chores while Paula and I had to clean this house from top to bottom?"

"Boys shouldn't do girl work," Gramps added.

Landry could only shake her head at her grandfather's comment. She should have expected it because she'd heard similar sentiments from him before. It still never ceased to amaze her.

"It's a different generation now, Gramps," Paula chimed in.

"Yeah, one where women are bringing home just as much money as the men. So if they can share in paying bills, they should be able to share doing chores too," Landry declared.

"Oh boy, she's definitely back," Dominic quipped. "Get out the soapbox."

Her brothers laughed but Landry wasn't surprised; the Norris boys always stuck together.

"Well if somebody has to say it, I guess it has to be me," Landry continued. "Women are always tasked with being independent and resourceful, while men get to work whichever jobs they want and then come home and sit on their butts."

Heinz Sr. shook his head and continued to eat his baked chicken as if he knew where this conversation was going. Astelle tended to her grandchildren and took small bites of the food on her plate.

"That's right. I take care of both my children and I work two jobs. Does that mean their father should be allowed to work his part-time fast-food shifts and then come home and lie on the couch for the remainder of the time?" Paula asked.

Geoffrey shook his head. "Nobody's saying all that."

"Good!" Paula exclaimed. "Because that's some bull and it's precisely why I sent him back home to his mama. I can do bad by myself."

"Takes some people longer to come to their true calling in life than others," Astelle finally spoke. "We should never be so quick or harsh to judge others."

"Oh goodness, she's going to the Bible," Paula whispered.

Astelle and Heinz Sr. heard her and sent warning glares her way, but Paula continued to eat, unbothered.

"So glad I'm in my own place and doing my own thing. I don't have to worry about the balance between men and women in relationships," Landry said.

"Hard work never hurt anybody," Astelle started. "Relationships are hard work, but they're worth it. Ain't that right, Heinz?"

Landry watched as her father nodded. "Absolutely right, my love," he said when he finished chewing.

Landry resisted the urge to frown. She'd had another try at the relationship thing, even if what she and Kristian were doing was a little on the strange side. Still, since coming home, she'd decided she could forego the entire game of love for the duration of her life if need be.

After a few hours had passed, first and second helpings of the meal were done and Gramps was already calling for his dessert. Regardless of their prior conversation Landry and Paula stood to help Astelle gather the dinner dishes and take them into the kitchen. Paula had taken the chocolate cake out to the dining room and Landry followed her with cake plates in one hand, a gallon of vanilla ice cream tucked uncomfortably under her arm and spoons in the other hand.

She'd just made it to the table when Paula started to yell. "Oh my! Oh my! Oh my!"

"What is that child yelling about now?" Gramps asked.

Giselle had gotten out of her chair to go to her mother's side, looking at her with curiosity as she continued to yell. Paula's oldest child was Charles Jr.; he was nine and not impressed by much of anything the adults in this family did or said. So he remained in his seat playing the handheld video game Landry had given him for his last birthday.

In seconds everybody, except Gramps, was up from the table, joining Paula where she was standing in front of the bay window. Heinz Jr. pulled the curtains all the way back and almost knocked over one of their mother's plants.

"Dayum!" Geoffrey crowed as he peered out the window and then bent down to scoop Giselle up in his arms. "Look at that limo."

"Who is that? Y'all invite somebody else to dinner?" Dominic asked.

"No," Astelle said, coming out of the kitchen. "I didn't invite anybody."

Landry hadn't moved. After putting the ice cream onto the cherrywood table covered in her mother's old lace tablecloth, she'd set the plates down slowly. The spoons were still in her hand when she chanced a look out the window. That's the precise moment her heart stammered in her chest.

It couldn't be.

No, she told herself. It wasn't.

He was thousands of miles away, running his island without her there to distract him. Kristian had let her walk out of his room and subsequently out of his life. She'd only spoken briefly to Malayka who didn't seem at all fazed by Landry's announcement that she was resigning and would send her a list of recommended stylists to choose from. Her flight had left the island later that morning and since then she had not heard from or seen anyone from the DeSaunters family.

"Somebody's gettin' out!" Giselle yelled.

"Oh my, he sure is," Paula stated. "He certainly…is."

Landry had already looked away from the window. Her heart was pounding in her chest and she chastised herself for being foolish. The fact was that her body was beginning to warm in a way it hadn't done since she'd been in Grand Serenity. She shook her head and was just about to walk back into the kitchen when Paula's next words stopped her.

"He's fine and he's walking up to our door like he owns this house and everyone in it. Oh my, let me get myself together," her sister said.

Landry knew.

Seconds after the doorbell rang and before she could wrap her mind around what was happening, he spoke.

"My name is Kristian DeSaunters and I'm looking for Landry Norris."

His words trickled through her like a good alcoholic beverage, warm, slow and potent as hell.

"How did you know to come to my parents' house? How did you even know who they were and where they lived?" Landry asked him an hour later, when he walked into her condo behind her.

"I did extensive research on you before you came to the island," he told her. "I thought we went over that already."

"You have people investigated, follow them when they are on your island and then hunt them down when they're not?"

He wouldn't say he'd hunted her down. Not exactly.

Yesterday afternoon, after a meeting with his father and having endured yet another sleepless night, Kris decided to make the trip to the United States. He'd waited long enough. Too long, as his brother and sister not-so-kindly put it.

"I needed to speak to you," was his reply.

Her tone was edgy and he was afraid there would be an argument instead of the calm, mature discussion he'd planned.

"You could have just called," she told him after she'd dropped her purse onto one of two white couches that faced each other.

There was a lot of white in there, the furniture, the huge crystal chandelier hanging from the white ceiling, the large piece of art on one side of the wall and the cheerful looking flowers in the crystal vases sitting on the iron-and-glass coffee table. He'd assumed she would have a brighter decor with colors that represented her vibrant personality. He'd been wrong about her yet again.

"I wanted to see you," he admitted.

Kris was here for one purpose and he was not going to be deterred, especially not by his own foolishness this time.

She stood near a wall with a silver mirror and a pale gray painted table, which held another vase with a burst of deep purple flowers. She liked fresh flowers, he deduced.

"I don't understand why," she replied honestly.

He could always expect that from Landry. Honest candor that he was certain didn't come easy to every person he'd meet in this world.

"I mean, when I left the island I was suspected of setting off a bomb in the palace," she continued, folding her arms behind her back as she leaned against the wall.

She wore blue slacks and a white blouse. One of the ones he'd bought for her as he recalled personally selecting this one with the navy blue stripes and swinging sleeves. There were thick bangles on her arms and a silver choker at her neck. She was still beautiful; that hadn't changed at all.

"Gary and Salvin found the man you heard talking on the phone," he began. He'd hoped to talk to her about all the drama that had ensued on the island after she'd left, later, but if she wanted to hear it now, he would definitely oblige.

"His name was Harry Copeland and he was posing as one of the construction crew that had been hired to work on some structural issues throughout the palace." Kris walked farther into the living area, but he did not take a seat on either of the couches.

She continued to stare at him. Kris was no stranger to people looking at him. That came with the title. Whether he was on a stage giving a speech, riding in a car or simply walking down the street, people looked. But none of them had any clue. Except for Landry. She'd seen through him from the very start.

"He knew about the ball and who would be there because he was working with Amari Taylor, Malayka's hairstylist. It had only taken an hour after reviewing the surveillance tapes and seeing Harry enter and exit that room next to Malayka's dressing room, for the guards to find him. He'd actually come back to the palace to resume working two days after the ball," Kris said with a shake of his head.

He and Gary had figured the guy was going to try again since none of the royal family had been injured in the explosion and they were almost certain that the DeSaunters family were the actual targets.

"Amari?" she asked. "He's such a...a colorful character."

Kris nodded. He thought something similar when he'd first met the man as well.

"Amari's not as talkative as Harry, but we've had them both in custody for over a week now. Malayka was livid when she found out. She explained that you and she had been going to the dressing room to discuss her gown the night of the ball, when she realized she'd lost one of her earrings. She went to her room to get another pair and you said you would meet her in the dressing room. Before you could get there Amari showed up. He's the one who hit you, but he's not saying why."

She appeared surprised and then irritated.

"Let me guess—your cameras picked that up too. Wow, I guess me leaving your room every morning wasn't as much of a secret as I thought it was. Someone was watching all along," she said with a shake of her head.

"Security is important," he told her. "As you can tell, even with all that we already had in place, we still need to step it up. Until we find out what's really going on between Amari and this Harry guy who we think is just a middleman, we're still being targeted."

"Why?"

He shook his head. "I'm not sure. It may be something related to the bank, hence the break-in there, but we're still trying to work that out."

She nodded then. "So why are you here if there's still

more to find out? I know you didn't come this far to tell me about Amari and his cohorts."

He hadn't; she was absolutely right about that. However, Kris wasn't sure how what he actually wanted to say was going to go over with her at this moment.

"No. I didn't," he finally said.

"Then what?"

It sounded like a dare. She'd stepped away from the wall and now had her arms by her sides. Her hair was pulled back into a messy ponytail; huge hoop earrings swung at her ears. She looked casual and classy all at the same time. Kris clenched his hands. He'd never been this nervous about anything in his life before. That's how he knew it was important.

It was very important.

That's why he decided to take a page from her book and just say it.

"I missed you," he told her. "I've never missed anyone in my life like this besides my mother. Every day, every hour of every day I missed you."

She did not move and did not speak.

"I ate pizza. You've been gone for fourteen nights and five of them I had pizza for dinner. I drank beer. In my room, of course, but so much beer. I'd hoped it would make me sleep better, but it didn't."

He took a breath and continued. This was uncomfortable and odd yet he knew it was the most important thing he'd ever do in his life.

"I heard every word you said that morning on my balcony and the many times before that. I didn't give us a chance. I never planned to entertain the idea of an 'us.' It's only a small consolation to know that you didn't either. But I should have. I should have known from the first time I looked at your pictures. You were different—I just wasn't prepared for how different."

Her arms fell to her sides.

"If I were a god with power over the entire universe I wouldn't deserve you. But I want you, Landry. I want the girl who was born in Northern Seton Hospital Center on February tenth, weighing eight pounds and three ounces. I want the girl who kicked the winning goal on her high school soccer team, and the young lady who aced all her classes for the first two years at California State Polytechnic University. And I want the woman who had *Harper's Bazaar* call her back for a second internship and then offer her a full-time job. I know that she's independent and headstrong and can be a little stubborn. But I want her. I love her."

For once in her life, Landry didn't know what to say.

She'd been listening to Kristian talk and watching him at the same time. He looked fabulous in his navy blue suit and light blue shirt. His tie was pink and blue and made his eyes look brighter. His shoes were shined, his hair cut close and shaped up precisely. He was every bit as handsome as she'd thought he was the first time she'd seen him.

And every bit as intimidating.

Why had he really come here? What did he want from her?

He said he loved her. Wasn't that something a woman usually wanted to hear?

Not her. Not now.

She was shaking her head as she started walking toward the door.

"Thank you for telling me that my name has been cleared and that your family no longer considers me a threat. I appreciate you coming all this way for that, but it wasn't necessary. I would have been fine with an email."

She was reaching for the doorknob when his hand covered hers. Landry looked up into his face; she saw a muscle twitch in his jaw, smelled the rich scent of his cologne.

"I couldn't do this in an email," he told her about two seconds before he grabbed her by the waist and pulled her close to him.

The kiss was fast, potent, pure fire.

Her arms wrapped around his neck as if they were always meant to be there and damn if she didn't give totally in to the kiss. She could have sworn she didn't want to, that this was against everything that she'd so fervently believed for so long. She was independent and successful; she did not need to be with a prince, of all people. She did not need the duties and responsibilities that would no doubt come with loving him. He wasn't like any other man and she knew that wasn't just because of the title. She knew and that fact had her pressing her body into his.

He turned them and her back was now against the door. His hands were moving up and down her sides as his tongue dueled dangerously and deliciously with hers. She was drowning; she could feel herself going slowly, but most definitely, under. When he cupped her bottom and lifted her off the floor, Landry sighed, her legs instantly going around his waist.

"Bedroom," he said between nipping little bites on her lower lip.

"Down the hall and to your right," she answered, her palms flattening on the back of his head as he walked.

He moved quickly which was a good and bad thing, because when he entered the room and dropped her onto the bed, Landry wanted to get up and run. Then she wanted to strip and beg.

"I don't know what's happening," she admitted, when he pulled his jacket off and tossed it on the floor.

"I didn't know either but now I'm convinced it's a good thing," he told her and worked on his tie and the first buttons of his shirt.

Landry lifted her blouse up and over her head, tossing it onto the floor the same way he'd done his jacket. She toed off her slip-on flats and then went to the buttons of her pants.

"How is this happening? How will it work?" she asked and then pushed her pants down her legs, letting them fall to the floor as well. "You live on an island and I live here. I have a business and clients and you have thousands of citizens to care for."

He'd removed his shirt and the undershirt he wore beneath it. He was unbuckling his pants when he looked up at her.

"I have a private jet. There's no reason you can't fly to where you need to be, when you need to be there. Detali has been fielding numerous calls from a diverse group of people interested in her designs. That's all thanks to you. Even Sam said she wished there were someone stationed on Grand Serenity who could bring more fashion icons to the attention of our residents."

Landry opened her mouth to say something and then she closed it again, because once more, she wasn't sure what to say.

"I don't... I mean, I can't," she stuttered.

He removed his shoes, his pants and then his boxers. After taking a few seconds to slip on a condom he had in his back pocket, he came closer to the bed; he planted a knee on the mattress between her legs and cupped her face in his hands. "You can do anything you want, from wherever you want, as long as you're with me. As long as I know that at night I can lie down beside you. That I can look into your eyes and tell you how much I love you. How much I need you in my life. Say you'll marry me."

The next kiss was shorter, yet it still took her breath away. He moved quickly to rid her of her bra and panties and then he was over her, sinking deep inside her before she could think of another question or argument.

Epilogue

Two weeks later
The First Royal Wedding

"I love you," Landry said as she stood across from Kristian beneath a trellis full of red begonias.

A few seconds ago her father had handed her off to Kristian, the smile on Heinz Sr.'s face so big Landry feared it might be permanently stuck that way. Her parents had been elated when two days after Kristian had appeared at their house, he was there once again to ask for Landry's hand in marriage.

Sure, it seemed fast. She'd known Kristian for three and a half months, but there wasn't a doubt in her mind that he was the man she wanted to marry.

Of course, Heinz Jr., her niece and nephew, her grandparents and the rest of her brothers were much more excited about getting an all-expenses-paid trip to Grand Serenity

Island. Paula was very interested in meeting Roland, in the hopes that the other prince didn't mind a ready-made family.

Planning a wedding in two weeks was not an easy feat but Sam had jumped right in and worked tirelessly to make this day everything Heinz and Astelle Norris had dreamed of for their oldest daughter. It was all so beautiful, Landry had to admit.

They'd chosen a spot outside the palace, close to the water and the path that led down to the abandoned stables. She'd known that would be important to Kristian as he'd admitted to only feeling close to his mother when he was there.

White chairs lined the lawn and accommodated the one hundred close family and friends that they'd decided to invite on such short notice. There were tall crystal vases at the end of each row of chairs filled to the point of bursting with blue jacaranda, bottlebrush and alpinia. Landry had selected the flowers herself, going for color and excitement as she, Paula and Sam wore all-white dresses.

Landry's dress had, of course, been made by Detali, her new favorite designer. While Peta insisted on making the bridesmaids gowns as soon as Landry told her about the wedding.

Prince Rafferty and Roland were in full regalia, their medals shined to perfection as each of them stood tall at the altar with Kristian.

As for her husband-to-be, Landry could only smile. He was temptingly gorgeous in his black jacket, the gold tassels at his shoulders and the sword at his hip giving him that dashing royal look without anyone even knowing his title. But it didn't matter what he was wearing to Landry. It only mattered what he said.

"I love you. Just you, for who and what you are," he whispered before the minister began the ceremony.

The rest of the day proceeded with all the pomp and circumstance of a royal wedding as Landry eagerly awaited the next morning when she would awake as Princess Landry Norris DeSaunters, owner and managing editor of the new magazine aptly titled *Tropical Fashions*. She was going to have her own magazine where she could focus on all things fashionable throughout the world. She and Sam were also working on a charity fashion show, which they hoped to make an annual event on the island.

Her parents had been right, Landry thought as she and Kristian took to the dance floor in the smaller ballroom inside the palace. She could have it all. She'd compromised by agreeing to move to Grand Serenity. But she didn't feel as if she'd sacrificed who and what she was to be with a man, not even to be with a prince.

* * * * *

*She's got sky-high ambitions to match the glamorous
penthouses she shows, but real estate agent
Angela Trainor keeps both feet firmly on the ground.
Her attraction to her sexy boss, Daniel Cobb, needs
to remain at bay or it could derail her promising
career. But when Daniel takes Angela under his wing,
their mutual admiration could become a sizzling
physical connection...*

*Read on for a sneak peek at
MIAMI AFTER HOURS,
the first exciting installment of
Harlequin Kimani Romance's continuity*
MILLIONAIRE MOGULS OF MIAMI!

"Now you just have to seal the deal and get to closing." He
knew that just because an offer had been made didn't mean
the sale was a foregone conclusion. Deals could fall apart
at any time. Not that it ever happened to him. Daniel took
every precaution to ensure that it didn't.

"Of course."

"Speaking of deals, I've recently signed a new client,
a developer that has tasked me with selling out the eighty
condos in his building in downtown Miami."

Angela's eyes grew large. "Sounds amazing."

"It is, but it's a challenge. The lower-end condos go for a thousand a square foot, and the penthouse is fifteen hundred a square foot."

"Well, if anyone can do it, you can."

Daniel appreciated her ego boost. "Thank you, but praise is not the reason I'm mentioning it."

"No?" She quirked a brow and he couldn't resist returning it with a grin.

"I want you to work on the project with me."

"You do?" Astonishment was evident in her voice.

"Why do you think I plucked you away from that other firm? It was to give you the opportunity to grow and to learn under my tutelage."

"I'm ready for whatever you want to offer me." She blushed as soon as she said the words, no doubt because he could certainly take it to mean something other than work. Something like what he could offer her in the bedroom.

Where had that thought come from?

It was his cardinal rule to never date any woman in the workplace. Angela would be no different. He didn't mix business with pleasure.

He banished the thought and finally replied, "I'm sure you are." Then he walked over to his desk, procured a folder and handed it to her. "Read this. It'll fill you in on the development. Let's plan on putting our heads together on a marketing strategy tomorrow after you've had time to digest it."

Angela nodded and walked toward the door. "And, Daniel?"

"Yes?"

"Thank you for the opportunity."

Don't miss MIAMI AFTER HOURS
by Yahrah St. John, available June 2017
wherever Harlequin® Kimani Romance™
books and ebooks are sold.

Get 2 Free Books,

Plus 2 Free Gifts —

just for trying the Reader Service!

KIMANI™ ROMANCE